Books by Ed Dunlop

The Terrestria Chronicles
The Sword, the Ring, and the Parchment
The Quest for Seven Castles
The Search for Everyman
The Crown of Kuros
The Dragon's Egg
The Golden Lamps
The Great War

Tales from Terrestria
The Quest for Thunder Mountain
The Golden Dagger
The Isle of Dragons

Jed Cartwright Adventure Series
The Midnight Escape
The Lost Gold Mine
The Comanche Raiders
The Lighthouse Mystery
The Desperate Slave
The Midnight Rustlers

The Young Refugees Series
Escape to Liechtenstein
The Search for the Silver Eagle
The Incredible Rescues

Sherlock Jones Detective Series
Sherlock Jones and the Assassination Plot
Sherlock Jones and the Willoughby Bank Robbery
Sherlock Jones and the Missing Diamond
Sherlock Jones and the Phantom Airplane
Sherlock Jones and the Hidden Coins
Sherlock Jones and the Odyssey Mystery

The 1,000-Mile Journey

The Golden Lamps

THE TERRESTRIA CHRONICLES: BOOK SIX

*An allegory
by Ed Dunlop*

cross & crown
PUBLISHING
RINGGOLD, GEORGIA

www.TalesOfCastles.com
Cover Art by Laura Lea Sencabaugh and Wayne Coley

The golden lamps : an allegory / by Ed Dunlop.
Dunlop, Ed.
[Ringgold, Ga.] : Cross and Crown Publishing, c2006
215 p. ; 22 cm.
Terrestria chronicles Bk. 6
Dewey Call # 813.54 ISBN 0978552350

After an attack on a small village by Argamor's
dark knights, the villagers petition King Emmanuel
to build them a castle for protection. The discovery
of mysterious golden lamps may spell doom for the
castle project.

Dunlop, Ed.
Middle ages juvenile fiction.
Christian life juvenile fiction.
Allegories.
Fantasy.

Printed and bound in the United States of America

That in all things

my King might have

the preeminence.

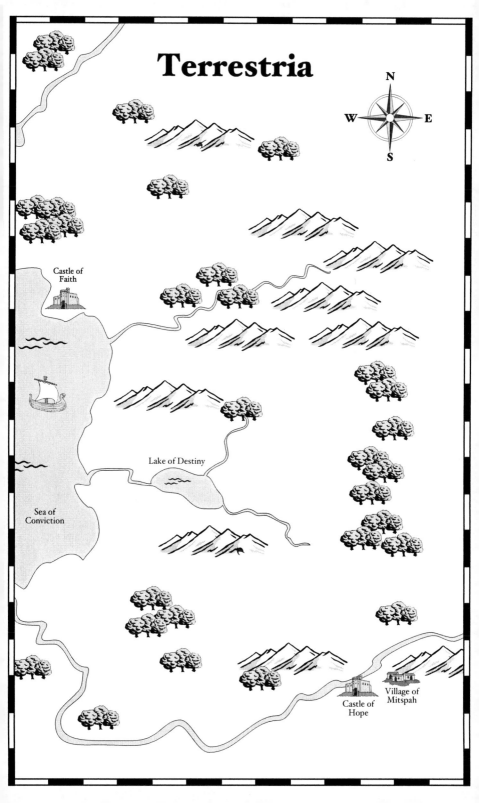

Terrestria

And he said unto them,

Take heed, and beware

of covetousness:

for a man's life

consisteth not in the

abundance of the things

which he possesseth.

— Luke 12:15

Prologue

The moon hung low in the heavens above the peaceful kingdom of Terrestria, a huge silver medallion resting against a backdrop of dark velvet. Stars glittered like tiny diamonds.

Rugged mountains, tall spires of rock sculpted by the wind to resemble the towers and turrets of an enormous castle, reached for the sky.

High on the mountainside, a lone wolf howled mournfully.

A dark shadow moved, hesitated, and then moved again.

Wispy fingers of cloud crept silently across the face of the moon, casting ominous shadows across the land. The wind howled softly, gently, as if in mourning. The wolf fell silent, head thrown back, studying the moon in bewilderment.

The clouds grew thicker, darker. The moon fought back, struggling to cast its silver beams across the land.

High on the mountainside, a huge opening suddenly loomed, as if the mountain had opened its mouth. Flickering amber light sprang from deep within the heart of the mountain, pulsing and throbbing with a peculiar tempo.

A shadow moved, and the dark silhouette of a powerful figure appeared at the cave's mouth. Glancing toward the opening, the figure turned and surveyed the hillside. With a gesture of determination, he raised his cape and swept it toward the heavens.

The clouds abruptly closed in front of the moon, obscuring its light as though the heavenly body were in the grip of a giant fist. The stars in the heavens winked out one by one, tiny candles snuffed out by the breath of an unseen being. Darkness swept across the land like a blanket pulled across a bed.

The figure turned and walked swiftly into the glowing cave. With the long strides of a man on a mission he hurried deep into the heart of the mountain. He paused and grunted in satisfaction when he came to a huge, snarling fire in the very center of the mountain, the source of the pulsing amber light.

Setting an enormous sack upon the floor of the cavern, he reached within its folds and produced a large, misshapen lump of molten gold. He then hurled it into the blazing fire and watched in delight as it softened and then began to change shape. Moments later, he reached bare-handed into the flames and retrieved the gold.

Working swiftly and deftly, he began to shape the gold with his hands. Squeezing gently with strong, gnarled fingers, he formed a handle, then a concave bowl, and then a long, tapered spout. He paused briefly to survey his work, grinned with pleasure, and then spoke to the object as if it were alive. "Excellent, my lovely one, you are exquisite."

His fingers flew as he spoke, forming delicate images of lilies, unicorns, swords and castles. "Ah, my lovely one, your beauty is exquisite, your allure irresistible, your sheen captivating. You shall indeed steal the hearts of men." He threw back his head and laughed. "You, as an instrument of light, shall instead become the instrument of darkness!"

Grinning evilly, he then carefully formed a delicate symbol upon the surface of the soft, lustrous metal: the image of a cross and a crown. "Together," he whispered, "we shall deceive Emmanuel's followers."

When the object was completed he set it carefully upon a rock ledge and then stepped back to examine and admire it. "Exquisite!" he boomed, "absolutely exquisite, my lovely one! And soon, you shall have a family."

Working swiftly at the blazing, snarling fire, the big craftsman fashioned numerous other lumps of molten gold into exquisite golden vessels until they were identical to the first. As he finished each one, he carefully placed it upon the rocky ledge beside the first. Within a matter of hours, the cavern was filled with dozens of the glittering golden lamps.

"Lovely ones, you are perfect!" the huge figure cried in delight. "You shall soon be free to do my bidding. Together, you and I shall capture the one golden object that rightfully belongs to me!"

With these words, he began to pick up the golden lamps and place them carefully about the cavern. When the vessels were arranged to his satisfaction he strode hurriedly down the rocky corridor and emerged on the hillside. Huge strides carried him down the steep slope.

Reaching the base of the mountain, he turned, raised his cape, and with a forceful gesture brought it swiftly down. A howling gust of wind swept down from the peaks above, powerful and chilling. The mountain trembled. A white-hot bolt of lightning slashed from the heavens and struck the ridge. Thunder roared. The mountain shook and the rocks trembled. With a roaring cacophony of sound that made it seem as if all of Terrestria were being destroyed, the mountain collapsed upon itself. The side of the mountain fell away, sliding downward with a thunderous roar and forever sealing off the entrance to the cavern.

The figure smiled in satisfaction. "Sleep, my lovely ones," he cried. "Take your rest. One day you shall be awakened by mortals, and then you shall do my bidding. Terrestria shall be ours."

Chapter One

The afternoon shadows were growing long as a band of dark knights charged swiftly up a steep, grassy slope above the little village of Hazah. "For Argamor!" they cried fiercely, and the hillside rang with the echoes of their determined voices. Swords raised, they dashed eagerly toward an outcropping of large sandstone boulders whose shape and arrangement gave the impression of a castle.

When the knights reached the ring of boulders, a band of King Emmanuel's knights appeared, eager to defend the ridge. "For the glory of Emmanuel!" the defenders cried as they raised their swords and shields. "For Emmanuel!" They hesitated for just a moment, and then swooped down as one upon the attackers.

The battle was fierce and the hillside rang with the sounds of the conflict. Sword met sword as the dark knights tried fiercely to take possession of the ridge while Emmanuel's men fought desperately to defend it. Rushing forward, the dark knights managed to penetrate the line of knights facing them and split the defending force in two. Within moments the defenders were scattered, each on his own, each finding himself facing at least two of the enemy. The situation was desperate.

Two dark knights descended on a tall, skinny warrior who had suddenly realized that he was cut off from the rest of the force. Swinging their swords fiercely they advanced slowly, steadily, knowing that their prey was cornered and that there would be no escape. The single knight glanced around quickly, desperately, knowing that he was outmatched. "Help me!" he cried to his companions, but there was no help at hand. Moments later, he lay motionless in the grass as the two dark knights raced to help their companions take the ridge.

One brave knight had charged fiercely at two dark knights, driving them backwards by the sheer force of his determination. He soon had them both pinned against the ring of boulders, but as his sword met the sword of his opponent the haft shattered and the blade went flying, leaving him defenseless. In a moment, he too lay dead in the grass.

Another defending knight, realizing the hopelessness of the situation, turned and ran for his life, but a deft blow from a broadsword dropped him lifeless in the grass.

The battle was over almost before it had started. Outnumbered and outmatched, King Emmanuel's knights simply could not defend the ridge against the ferocity of the invaders. As the last of the royal knights fell to the swords of Argamor's men, the band of dark knights gave a lusty cheer. "The battle is ours!" they cried in delight. "We took the ridge!" Raising their swords high, they stepped over the bodies of their fallen adversaries and celebrated their victory.

"Well done, dark knights," a tall, broad-shouldered man in woodsman's clothing called as he hurried down the slope toward them. "Without question, the battle is yours." The band of dark knights grinned broadly at his words. They rushed up the hillside to meet him, clustering eagerly around him as they reached him.

The tall man gave a look of disdain at the bodies lying motionless in the grass. He made a sweeping gesture across the hillside with the gnarled staff in his hand. "Emmanuel's men, gather round," he called. "Let's evaluate the battle and see wherein your errors lie."

With groans of dismay and expressions of shame, the dead knights came to life, standing to their feet and starting slowly up the steep slope. "Look lively," the man cried. "Just because you lost the skirmish doesn't mean that you have to walk like dead men."

The band of dark knights laughed at this, but the tall man silenced them with a stern look.

As the defeated knights reached him the tall man dropped to his knees in the grass. "Gather round."

Dropping their wooden swords and shields in the grass, the knights sank to sitting positions in a loose circle around the tall man with the victors on his right and the defeated force on his left. "We were outnumbered, Paul," one knight complained. "There were twice as many of them. We didn't have a chance!"

"Never say that," the woodsman growled, giving the speaker a stern look. "You are King Emmanuel's men! Your strength comes not from your numbers, for His Majesty does not limit himself in such a fashion."

Paul's expression suddenly softened as he surveyed the defeated knights before him, for in reality they were young boys ranging from ten to twelve years of age. "You fought hard, men, but you lost to Argamor's forces and you lost rather quickly. Now—do any of you know why you lost?"

"They had more men than we did," one lad replied. "It was two to one, Paul."

"Forget how many men either side had," Paul said in

exasperation. "That's not why the battle was won or lost. You made several errors, and the dark knights took advantage of them and won the skirmish." He looked from one boy to another. "Do you know what you did wrong?"

The boys were silent, most with their heads down, a few studying the face of the tall woodsman.

"First of all," Paul said, raising his voice, "you forgot that you were defending a castle. Why did you leave the boulders and race down to meet the attackers on their own level? You had the advantage when you were on the high ground, yet you voluntarily left that and came down to meet Argamor's men. That was your first mistake.

"Your second mistake: you allowed the dark knights to divide your force so that each of you was fighting alone, rather than staying unified and fighting together. There is strength in unity, gentlemen. When you become knights and engage in real battles, you will learn to fight for each other and fight together. A warrior who fights by himself is easily defeated."

The boys were silent as they pondered his words.

"There were other mistakes," Paul continued, "but for now I want you to focus on just those two. I want you to learn two things from this skirmish. One, anytime you hold the high ground you hold the advantage. Defend it, fight for it, hold it. A castle gives a huge advantage to those who hold it. Two, always remember that you fight for each other; you never fight alone. United, you stand. Divided, you fall."

He looked around the circle of young would-be knights. "Are there any questions?"

The boys were silent.

"No questions? Then let's go to battle again. Same places as before."

"Can't we be Emmanuel's knights this time?" a tall boy among the dark knights asked. "I don't like being Argamor's knight. I hate shouting 'For Argamor!' Can't we switch places?"

Several of his companions nodded in agreement.

The tall woodman smiled. "I'm glad you feel that way, Marcus, for there is nothing worse than serving Argamor. You understand, of course, that you are merely playing a part as we run through these skirmishes in order to train for real battle. We all know that you would rather be on Emmanuel's side, but just for the moment, play the part of a dark knight, would you? We'll switch places next time."

The boy nodded.

Paul stood. "All right, men, let's run through it again. Emmanuel's men, to your places behind the boulders. Don't forget that you are defending a castle. Argamor's men, take your places at the bottom of the hill. Attack when you are ready."

He turned and walked up the slope to a position some twenty paces above the ring of boulders. The band of dark knights walked to the bottom of the slope as Emmanuel's knights took up positions behind the boulders.

As Paul took a seat on a fallen log, a small man wearing a magnificent scarlet doublet and a cloak of black and purple dropped to a seat beside him. "The boys fight well, Paul. One day they will make excellent knights."

Paul nodded. "Aye, they take it seriously, Demas. These boys put their whole hearts into this training, and for that very reason they will, as you say, one day make excellent knights for His Majesty."

"For Argamor!" a young voice cried, and the battle began anew.

The two men watched in silence as the band of dark knights charged up the grassy hillside, wooden swords held aloft, their faces grimacing in determination. Behind the boulders, the smaller band of young knights crouched eagerly, gripping their swords in anticipation. Demas laughed. "They do put their whole hearts into this, don't they? It's most amusing to watch."

Paul shook his head as he threw a glance at his friend. "There's nothing amusing about it, Demas. The youth of Terrestria are the future of this kingdom, and both Argamor and King Emmanuel know that very well. One day these lads will be swinging steel swords rather than wood, my friend, and the battles they will face will not be mock skirmishes. They had better be prepared."

Demas' face showed that he had taken offense. "You know what I mean, Paul."

Below them, the battle raged.

Paul pointed. "Watch Andrew. He has the heart of a lion, and his sword shows it. I'd hate to face him in battle once he has completed training and is wielding a real sword."

Demas snorted. "Aye. If only his older brother had half the heart he does."

The tall woodsman gave him a puzzled glance. "You really don't like Phillip, do you?" He laughed. "You had better learn to like him, Demas, seeing he's to be your son-in-law."

The other man shrugged. "That may not happen. I haven't yet given him permission to marry Rebecca."

"Why not? The boy's been courting her for nearly two years now. The entire village knows that they have eyes only for each other. Phillip has won your daughter's heart, Demas."

"The boy is a peasant, the son of a peasant. Rebecca is the daughter of a successful merchant."

"Is he not a good man? Would you deny Rebecca her happiness simply because Phillip comes from a poor family?"

Demas shrugged and threw up his hands as if to defend himself. "I only want to be certain that he can support my daughter properly. The lad shows no initiative, Paul, no drive to succeed." He glanced toward the mock battle taking place down below. "If only he were more like his little brother, Andrew. Now there's a lad who shows promise."

"Their father has been dead for nearly five years, Demas. Phillip has supported his mother and his brother all that time, though he was barely fourteen when he lost his father—how much more initiative do you want? How do you want the boy to prove himself?"

"I've asked him to present me with the price of a horse," his friend explained. "If he can save enough to buy a horse, he will have shown that he has enough initiative to support my daughter properly, and at that time I will give permission for them to marry."

"You are asking for a dowry? You would sell your daughter for the price of a horse?"

Demas had suddenly become red-faced. "Nay, I didn't say that!" he roared. "I merely asked the lad to prove himself to me by saving that amount."

"You will keep the money, of course."

Demas gave an angry nod.

Paul studied the combatants below for several seconds and then turned to his friend. "Phillip has supported his mother and brother for nearly five years now. I'd say he has made a fair show of his initiative. Why not let them marry?"

"The lad is a peasant, Paul, and the son of a peasant. Rebecca is the daughter of a successful crockery merchant."

"A successful crockery merchant who cannot afford a horse," Paul replied with a laugh, though not in derision. "Though if Phillip proves himself, you will have one soon enough."

Demas' jaw tightened in anger, but he said nothing.

Paul was thoughtful. "Perhaps your focus is on the wrong things, Demas. Phillip comes from a poor family, but he is a young man of character. He is honest, diligent in his business, compassionate toward others. I would be proud to have him as a son-in-law."

His companion shrugged.

"Material possessions are not the most important things in this life, yet you have asked him to prove himself in those matters, as if these were the things that really mattered."

"Possessions do matter," Demas argued. "A man must support his family."

"Aye, of course," Paul replied. "You have done that. I have done that. And, you must admit, young Phillip has also done that."

The other snorted. "Phillip and his family live like peasants."

"They are peasants, Demas. You and I are peasants. We live in a village of peasants, though it is a simple matter to tell that you desire more."

"A man must set goals, Paul, make something of himself. And I simply ask the same of any man who requests the hand of my daughter in marriage."

"Aye, my friend, of course. A man must set goals. But when a man sets goals that are beyond his reach and he then becomes consumed with reaching them, those goals become his master and he becomes their slave. Is that not perhaps where you now find yourself?"

"King Emmanuel has not forbidden the possession of wealth," Demas retorted.

"Aye, but he has warned us in the book that we must not love wealth," the tall woodsman cautioned. "He told us that the love of wealth becomes the root of all evil."

Demas didn't answer.

The sounds of the mock battle below caught their attention and they both turned to watch the skirmish. The dark knights had divided their forces and were attacking the sandstone ridge from two sides. Emmanuel's men were still in possession of the ridge and were holding their own.

Demas looked at the sky, noting that dark clouds were rolling in from the north and that a brisk wind was beginning to blow, swirling fallen leaves about in tight circles and making the grass on the hillside dance like the waves of the ocean. "It looks like we're in for a storm."

"Watch this, Demas."

As the men watched, six or eight dark knights suddenly swept around the end of the outcropping and charged across the hillside above the boulders, then dashed down toward the defenders, attacking them from above.

"They listened to the strategy you gave Emmanuel's knights," Demas observed, "and they're using it against them."

Paul nodded.

The attack from above was unexpected, but the defenders quickly rallied their troops and swiftly repelled the attack. The dark knights retreated, leaving two men lying in the grass. Emmanuel's knights started to give chase and then thought better of it, returning quickly to the safety of the ring of boulders.

Paul nodded, pleased at what he saw. "They're learning."

"They have a good teacher," Demas observed.

Paul stood. "Well, enough for today. Let's bring the battle to a close and head for home, shall we? I'm certain that our young knights have chores waiting at home."

The tall woodsman strode into the center of the fray, holding up both hands and calling, "That's enough for today, lads. Let's call a truce, shall we?" He surveyed the battlefield. "It looks like Argamor's forces lost four men in this battle, while Emmanuel lost only two. Well done, men. You followed instructions and you were successful in defending the castle. Gather round. I want to give you one or two more pointers and then we'll all head for home."

Paul knelt in the grass and the young would-be knights formed a circle around him. Demas stood to one side, quietly observing.

"Both sides fought well, men, and you are to be commended. Emmanuel's men, you followed my instructions, and therefore you were able to defend the castle, though you were facing a force larger than your own. Remember the two things—"

"Paul!" One of the boys interrupted in an attempt to get the woodsman's attention.

"Just a moment, David. Let me finish."

Another boy rose to his knees, pointing across the valley. "Sire, look! Who are those men?"

Paul turned and looked in the direction that the boy indicated, and his heart leaped in fear. On the crest of the ridge to the north, just three or four furlongs from the village, three dark knights on horseback had crossed a narrow space between the trees. As he watched in consternation, two more knights rode into view.

Paul turned to the boys. "How many knights did you see?"

David's face was filled with fear. "At least a score, sire, maybe more. Maybe as many as thirty."

The tall man leaped to his feet. "They're preparing to attack Hazah! Lads, run home as fast as you can! Quickly, now, find your fathers and tell them what is happening!"

The boys scattered like leaves before a brisk wind. Paul turned to Demas. "Let's warn the village. That which I feared most is upon us, and Hazah is not prepared."

Chapter Two

The attackers rode swiftly down upon the sleepy village of Hazah. Fifty riders dressed in the dark armor of Argamor rode at full gallop down the tree-shrouded slope to the north of the town.

Confusion reigned in the village as the tower gong sounded the alarm. Women screamed, men shouted, and children cried. Dogs barked and barked, sensing that something was amiss, while donkeys brayed in fear. The villagers were confused and terrified, totally unprepared for the attack and uncertain as to what to do.

Merchants dropped their shutters and bolted their doors. Housewives ran into the streets, searching for their children. Farmers left their fields and dashed for home, some attempting to take their animals with them, others leaving all and running for the safety of the eight-foot wooden palisade that surrounded the little town.

The village reeve appeared, wringing his hands and peering about in fear, uncertain what course of action to take.

"Close the gates!" Paul cried to the reeve and to the other villagers as he scrambled down from the tower where he had rung the warning gong. "Get the women and children inside!"

The reeve ran to the gate and was met by another villager. Together, they hastily swung the gates closed and prepared to bar them. "Wait!" a voice cried in terror. "Let me in!" The reeve opened the gate for an instant to admit a terrified farmer.

Argamor's men rode into the clearing at that instant. A lone farmer ran desperately for the gate, but one of the dark knights raised a crossbow and dropped him with one shot. The reeve's mouth dropped open, and he stood, unable to move, transfixed with horror.

Paul dashed past him and slammed the gate closed. Two men thrust the bars into place.

The men of the village had armed themselves with an assortment of hay rakes, axes, and shovels, and they began to gather at the gate.

"We must not go against such an enemy with self-styled weapons such as these," Paul told them. "Only the sword of Emmanuel is effective against Argamor's forces."

"I must protect my shop," one man ventured. "Everything I own is there."

"These barbarians will not steal from me," another said.

"We must protect what is ours," said a third.

Paul raised his voice. "Men of Hazah, your first priority is to protect your families. Go home. Make certain that your wives and children are safe within your walls. Stand at the door, guard them with your lives, and petition King Emmanuel for his protection. He is our only hope at a time such as this."

"Michael, come back here!" a woman's voice screamed, and the men turned to see a young boy climbing up into a tree that leaned out over the palisade wall.

"Ginger is out there!" the boy cried. "I have to get my dog!"

"Son, come back," a man called, but it was too late. The boy had already dropped over the wall. A moment later, a scream of horror gave witness to the cruelty of the dark knights.

A barrage of arrows soared over the palisade wall, missiles of death and destruction. "To your homes!" Paul cried. "Protect your families!"

Two of Argamor's horsemen rode forward and threw ropes around the tops of the logs of the palisade. Turning their mounts, they rode away, pulling down an entire section of the palisade. The village wall was breached.

Spurring their mounts forward, the invaders rode into the village. Shouting and laughing, the dark knights rode swiftly through the narrow streets of the little village, hurling burning torches onto the thatched roofs of the houses and shops. Within moments, the village was aflame. Wheeling their sturdy horses, the attackers rode away as swiftly as they had come.

A young girl ran screaming down the street. One dark rider leaned low in the saddle, seized the sleeve of her gown, and hefted her up across the neck of his mount. Demas bellowed with rage and charged after the horseman. "You bring my daughter back here!"

The dark knight turned, and knowing that the little merchant was helpless to stop him, mocked him as he rode away. As the powerful warhorse shot through the opening in the palisade wall, a lone arrow sped through the air, striking the warrior at the base of the neck just below his helmet. The dark knight tumbled from the saddle, taking his screaming young captive with him. His horse raced on without him.

Paul ran forward. He snatched the girl from the grasp of the dark knight who lay motionless upon the ground. The child wrapped her arms around his neck.

"She's all right," the tall woodsman called to Demas and

his wife, as the anxious parents ran forward. "She is all right." He handed the sobbing young girl to Demas, who seized her eagerly and then broke into tears.

"Save your homes!" Paul called to the villagers. "The riders have gone, but save your homes from the flames!"

Men dashed to the village well. Confusion reigned as they all attempted to seize the one wooden bucket.

At that moment, huge drops of rain began to spatter down upon the dusty streets of the little village, falling slowly at first and then faster and faster. Abruptly, the clouds ripped open in a torrential downpour, instantly dousing the flames that raged upon the rooftops.

"Praise the name of King Emmanuel!" a woman cried. "He has sent the rain and saved our village!" The villagers danced in the streets for joy, hands raised in the air as the rain splashed down upon their faces. Moments later, the clouds abruptly parted and golden sunlight streamed down like a beam of promise and hope.

Paul looked around at the villagers who were gathering in the street. "Where is the archer who saved Mira? Who fired the arrow that killed the horseman?"

A young man stepped forward with a longbow in his hand. "I did, sire."

Paul was stunned. "Phillip!" He turned and looked at Demas, who met his gaze for a moment and then turned away.

"We must be prepared for the next attack," the reeve told the villagers who were assembled in the town square that evening. "Today only two of our number were killed, but it could have been much worse. But for Phillip's quick action with his bow, Mira would have been taken captive, and had not our good King sent the rain, we all know that Hazah would have been destroyed."

He bowed his head. "As the village reeve, I must beg your pardon. It was my duty to make certain that the town was protected, but I must confess that I have shirked that duty."

He paused and looked from one face to another. "The very name of our town is an indication of our sad state of affairs. 'Hazah' in the ancient language means 'to sleep,' and that is exactly what we as a village have been doing. His Majesty has warned us to be vigilant and watchful, lest the enemy attack us, yet I fear that we have not paid heed. But for the flimsy palisade around our village, we have made no preparations. We were totally unprepared for what happened today. Do you realize that almost none of us had swords with which to defend ourselves? That must change."

"Paul has been trying to warn us that something like this could happen," a man spoke up.

"Except for our woodsman friend," the reeve paused and smiled at Paul, "none of us has taken the threat seriously. We have been asleep, oblivious to the dangers we face as a village. As you know, Paul has been training our boys in swordsmanship and battle tactics that they might one day become knights in His Majesty's service. Even so, we have not taken him or his words seriously."

"Why would Argamor attack our little village?" a farmer asked. "We have nothing that he wants."

The reeve spread his hands in a gesture of frustration. "I do not know, my friend. I have been asking myself the same question."

Paul stood up. "Do you not realize why Hazah is important to our adversary?" he asked with a note of disbelief in his voice. "Our little village is made up for the most part of young families. Families with children and young people." He looked around at his fellow villagers. "Aye, there is something here that Argamor wants—he wants our children! He knows that our children are the future of Emmanuel's kingdom—His Majesty himself told us that his kingdom is made up of such— and Argamor will attempt to seize the kingdom by capturing the hearts of the children."

He paused. "Did not one of the riders attempt to capture one of our children and ride off with her?"

There was a murmur of assent as the townspeople considered his words. Paul sat down.

"I have called this town meeting tonight," the reeve said, "in order that we might discuss our preparations for the future. As you may know, six men are on guard this very minute. I would suggest that we need to continue this practice. But we need to protect our little town in better ways than this."

He sighed. "Friends and neighbors, tonight is my last night as your reeve. After what happened today I feel that I must resign and allow you to choose someone more capable."

"Whom would we choose?" a man asked. "None of us would be any more capable than you."

"I would suggest that you choose Paul," the reeve replied. "He has already proven himself." He turned to the woodsman. "Paul, if these good people approve it, would you be willing to serve as our reeve?"

Paul considered the idea for a moment. "I will do my best," he replied simply.

"Good people of Hazah, will you have Paul as your reeve? I have already resigned, so right now you have no one."

A chorus of "ayes" followed.

"There you have it, my friend. You are the new reeve. This town meeting is now yours." The man stepped away.

Paul advanced slowly to the front. "Thank you, my friends, for your trust in me," he said quietly, "though I must admit that this takes me by surprise. As I said, I will do my best."

"What are we going to do, Paul?"

"How are we going to protect ourselves?"

"Do you think the riders will come again?" The questions were coming fast and furious.

Paul held up both hands as if to fend off the questions. "My friends, one at a time, please! First of all, Matthias, our former reeve, is right—we must keep men on guard from now on. Six are guarding tonight, and we will select their replacements before we adjourn this meeting. I will serve as one of the relief guards tonight. We will serve in rotating shifts. During the daylight hours, two watchmen should be sufficient.

"Tomorrow at first light we shall bury our two fallen comrades and the dark knight, and then we shall form a thatching party to repair the damaged buildings. I want everyone there, whether or not your home or shop was damaged. If we work together we should be able to complete the work quickly. The damage was minimal to most buildings because King Emmanuel sent the rain in such a timely fashion. Praise his majestic name."

The townspeople gave voice to their assent.

"And now to make plans for the future," Paul continued. "We all agree that what happened today must never happen again. We must be prepared to defend our homes and our families." He paused and looked from one person to another. "Are we all in agreement?"

Without exception, the townspeople nodded and voiced their approval.

"First, we must petition His Majesty for weapons," Paul told them. "Each of us must have the sword of Emmanuel, and we must learn how to use it. Had we actually battled the dark knights this afternoon, our hay rakes and shovels would have been no match for their swords and crossbows."

Paul paused again. "And secondly, we must petition His

Majesty to build us a castle."

"A castle?" one farmer repeated.

"A castle!" The woman was incredulous.

"Would King Emmanuel build us a castle?"

The crowd erupted with exclamations of surprise and disbelief, and Paul waited until the excitement had abated somewhat. "Argamor's attacks upon our village are going to come more and more often, and become more and more vicious. We all saw this afternoon just how treacherous he and his followers can be.

"A castle is the only way that this valley and this village can be adequately protected," Paul continued. "We must band together as a village and send a petition to His Majesty, entreating him to build us a castle."

"Who would pay for this castle?" The question came from Demas. "The village is made up for the most part of peasants, Paul, and as you would know, the building of a castle is quite an undertaking. How would it be funded?"

"I believe that His Majesty himself would provide the materials," Paul replied slowly, thoughtfully, "though I think that he would expect us to provide most of the labor."

"Few of us are skilled in building," Demas argued, "and certainly none of us know anything of the building of a castle."

"Aye, but the building would be Emmanuel's project. We would ask him to send master architects and carpenters to train us. If we are willing, perhaps he could use us in the building of it."

"What about our own affairs?" Demas wanted to know. "A castle could take years to build. Are we to simply neglect our own business to attend to castle building?"

Paul held up his hands. "Again, His Majesty would decide how it is to be done. He knows our needs better than we do."

Paul looked around. "Let's discuss this, my friends. Are we in agreement—do we all see the need to petition His Majesty for a castle?"

"Perhaps there would be a simpler, easier way, Paul," a craftsman suggested. "Perhaps we could reinforce the existing palisade—make it sturdier and taller."

"We all know now that the present one is far from adequate," a voice observed.

Several voices expressed interest in the idea of reinforcing the existing palisade or building a newer, sturdier one.

"No wooden palisade, no matter how strong or how tall, can ever offer the protection that a stone castle offers," Paul reasoned. "A wooden palisade, as we saw today, can be pulled down by riders on horses."

"We'll build it much sturdier," the miller called.

"No matter how sturdily we build it, it can always be burned down, whereas stone walls will not burn."

"How much would a castle cost?"

"Well," the new reeve replied, "my friend Demas is right: a castle would be very costly to build. Such a project would require huge amounts of stone and mortar, vast supplies of timber, and much iron hardware. It would take months, and maybe years to build, and undoubtedly we would be the ones providing the bulk of the labor. For a time, it would interrupt our lives, our businesses, our schedules. There is no question about it—building a castle to protect our village and our families would be a very costly undertaking and we must be ready to sacrifice. Perhaps we as a village are not ready to pay so high a price.

"On the other hand, think of the price we paid this very afternoon. Two lives were lost because we were not prepared for Argamor's attack. Thomas and Marcella lost their precious son, Michael; Deborah lost her dear husband, Anthony."

Thomas and Marcella had their arms around each other. At the mention of the loss of their son they began to sob quietly.

Paul paused and looked at the tired faces of his fellow villagers. "My friends, are we willing to pay such a price again? I think not. And remember, next time the price could be even higher. Aye, a castle will be costly, but refusing to build one could be far costlier."

"What if His Majesty will not build us one?" The question came from one of the women.

"Our blessed King knows our needs and he will respond to our petitions in our best interests," the tall woodsman said quietly. "All we can do is send a petition and seek his will in the matter. I, for one, am willing to trust the matter to his hands and simply wait for his decision. My King has never failed me."

"I also am willing to trust His Majesty's decision," came a voice from the back of the assembly.

"And I," repeated several voices.

"Are we ready to send a petition to King Emmanuel, asking him to build us a castle, but knowing what it may cost us?"

"Aye," replied most of those present.

"Are we ready to commit ourselves heart and soul to this project? For really, that is what it will require."

Again, most responded in the affirmative.

"Are there those of us who are opposed to it?" Paul asked quietly.

"Perhaps some of us need more time to think it through," Demas replied. "This is a big decision and a big undertaking. Let's not rush into this too hastily."

"What if we discuss this further when we break for the noon meal tomorrow?" Paul suggested. "That will give us a bit of time to think it through and discuss it with our families. Fair enough?"

Demas nodded. "That's fair enough." Other villagers also nodded.

Paul looked across the weary group of villagers. "This has been a very difficult day, my friends, and many of you are very tired. We have a lot of work to do tomorrow. Let's get some rest."

As the villagers dispersed to their separate dwellings, no one noticed the two dark knights who stood on the ridge above the village, silently watching their every move.

Chapter Three

"So tell me what was decided in the meeting this afternoon," Rebecca pleaded, her dark eyes searching Phillip's face for clues. "The women weren't allowed in the meeting, and I haven't heard anything so far. You must tell me."

Phillip picked up an acorn and flicked it down the hill with his thumb and forefinger. "There's really not much to tell," he replied, doing his best to keep a straight face. "We discussed how well the thatching is progressing, which buildings we're going to repair tomorrow, that sort of thing. It was a rather dull affair."

"But what about the plans for a castle?" Rebecca asked eagerly. "Has anything been decided?"

"A castle?" Phillip acted perplexed. "What castle?" From their vantage on the hillside high above the town he and Rebecca could see for miles. He leaned forward as if greatly interested in something on the far side of the river.

Rebecca was exasperated. "The castle we were talking about last night! The castle that Paul thinks the town needs to build. The castle that everyone has been talking about today, all day. That castle!"

"Oh, that castle. Come to think of it, I guess we did discuss that castle for a moment or two."

"What was decided, Phillip?" Rebecca was nearly beside herself with curiosity. "Are we going to petition King Emmanuel for a castle or not?"

Phillip paused, mentally counting to ten before answering. He loved teasing Rebecca, and he was enjoying the moment immensely. "A decision was reached, of course, but I'm not sure that I'm supposed to tell anyone."

"Phillip!"

Phillip grinned. "All right, all right. I suppose I shouldn't tease you so much. But I only do it because I love you."

"If you loved me any more I couldn't bear it," Rebecca responded. "Now, tell me before I burst with curiosity—are we going to have a castle?"

"The decision is up to His Majesty, of course," Phillip began, intending to stall for just another minute, but at the look on his sweetheart's face he decided it was safest to move more rapidly. "Aye, the village is going to petition King Emmanuel to build us a castle."

The girl gave a squeal of delight. "Oh, I had hoped for it! Paul says that the village will be far safer when we have a castle."

"We have to wait and see what Emmanuel decides," he reminded her.

"I know, but you heard what Paul said: King Emmanuel will decide in our best interests. That means that he will build us a castle."

"Only if that is best for the town."

"Aye, but if we are safer with a castle, doesn't that mean that Emmanuel will agree?"

Phillip shrugged. "It's his decision, Rebecca."

The girl was thoughtful. "When will we send the petition?"

Phillip picked a blade of grass and twirled it between his thumb and finger. "Paul and some of the men are writing it up right now. I think they're planning to send it this very evening."

She looked deeply into his eyes. "You were brave to shoot that enemy knight to save Mira. Everyone says that you are a hero, you know. That's all the townspeople were talking about today. That and the plans for the castle, of course."

Phillip shrugged. "I didn't do it to be a hero; I did it to save your sister's life."

Rebecca gave him a radiant smile. "I know, my love, and thank you. Thank you from the bottom of my heart."

Phillip laughed. "You've already thanked me at least a dozen times today."

She laughed with him. "I know, but once more won't hurt, will it? My entire family is grateful." She looked up at him tenderly. "You made a real impression on my father yesterday. I could tell that he was deeply moved by your bravery."

A thoughtful look crossed her pretty face. "Perhaps now he will give permission for us to wed."

Phillip sighed. "That will take a miracle, Rebecca."

"Aye, but maybe yesterday was our miracle," she replied. "Father came home and wept as he told us what you had done. Your actions touched him, Phillip, touched him deeply, perhaps more than either of us will ever know."

Phillip looked at the sun. "We'd better head for home, Rebecca. I should have had you back ten minutes ago."

He helped her to her feet. "Thank you for sharing a few moments of your day with me, fair maiden. Your lovely presence is akin to the aroma of violets in the spring sunshine."

She laughed merrily as they trekked down the hillside. "And I thank you, brave sire, for accompanying me on this quest. I also enjoyed the time immensely. Though I must say," she intoned darkly, "that you did take a bit too long in telling me the town's decision regarding the castle."

He chuckled. "You must admit, though, fair maiden, that it was more fun this way."

She glanced at him admiringly. "Those who saw it happen say that it was an incredible shot that saved Mira. How did you become such an accomplished archer?"

Phillip shrugged. "Papa was an expert archer, one of the best bowmen in King Emmanuel's army. He taught me when I was very young."

He sighed. "I wish Papa were here now."

Rebecca gave him a tender smile in reply.

"Our petition to His Majesty," Paul said quietly, holding aloft a tightly rolled parchment. He looked around at the small group of villagers gathered with him on the hillside overlooking the town, and then he opened his hand, releasing the parchment. All eyes were on the parchment as it shot from his hand to disappear over the crest of the ridge to the north. "Our request is now in the throne room in the Golden City of the Redeemed," Paul observed. "Soon we will know the will of our King regarding the building of a castle."

The little group stood silently surveying the village for a moment or two, each deep in thought. "We might as well head for home," Paul said. The group followed him down the hill.

"How much longer until the thatching is done?"

"Two days at most," the tall woodsman replied. "Everyone is participating and the work is going quickly. If Emmanuel is pleased to hold the rains for two more days, we should be finished, which will be a blessing."

"How long will it be until His Majesty responds to our request for a castle?" another asked.

Paul shook his head. "There is no way to know, Jeruch. The matter is in Emmanuel's hands now. He will answer when he is ready."

A fortnight later three tall ships sailed slowly up Distinction River just before sunset. Curious, many of the townspeople gathered on the riverbank and watched in fascination as the vessels anchored in the middle of the river. The decks of the ships were alive with activity as the sails were lowered and stowed and the anchors were secured.

"Who are these people, Papa?" a child asked in a small voice. "Why are they coming here?"

"I don't know, Sweetheart," the father answered, "but we'll soon find out."

"They're lowering a boat," a little boy observed, pointing in excitement. "There are nine men in it. They're coming to see us!"

Moments later the boat grated on the gravel bar at the river's edge. The first man ashore was tall and stately, dressed in the clothing of a workman, but with the manner and bearing of a nobleman. His lively eyes and energetic step suggested that he was quite young, but his graying hair and beard told otherwise. "Greetings, good people of Hazah," he called as he approached the crowd on the riverbank. "I come in the name of His Majesty, King Emmanuel, Lord of Terrestria."

Paul had just joined the villagers, and now he stepped forward. "Welcome, my lord, to Hazah, where you will find a warm welcome since you come in the name of our gracious King. I am Paul, newly chosen reeve of the village."

"I am James of Arwyn, master engineer in the service of His Majesty," the nobleman replied.

"I have heard of you," Paul said. "You are said to be a man of great skill."

"I have been commissioned by King Emmanuel to select a site and build a castle for his glory and honor and for the protection of your village. With me is my staff of master craftsmen, ready to assist in the building."

The townspeople cheered at these words.

Master James smiled. "It seems we have quite an enthusiastic welcome."

Paul shook his hand. "We are delighted that you and your men are here, my lord. You bring glad tidings, for did I not understand you to say that His Majesty has approved the building of our castle?"

Master James nodded. "That's why we are here, Paul. His Majesty has indeed granted your request for a castle."

The townspeople gathered eagerly around Master James and his men, shaking their hands and welcoming them to the village. After initial introductions had been made, they began to ply the man with questions.

"Where will the castle be located?"

"How long will it take to build?"

"How can we help?"

Laughing, Paul stepped between the engineer and the villagers. He held up both hands. "Let's let Master James and his men get ashore before we put them to work, shall we? The first item of business is to welcome all the men ashore, help them get settled in, and feed them. Later we can ask our questions about the castle."

Master James smiled. "Thank you, my friend."

"Let's get the rest of your crew ashore and help them find lodging," Paul suggested. "After that we will put on a grand feast to welcome you properly to our village."

"My men and I will stay aboard ship until we can build barracks for our housing," the engineer replied. "We will not put any of your people out of their homes. But we will be grateful to dine with you."

The moon was just beginning to poke its silvery face above the ridges to the east as the people of Hazah assembled in the village square. They chattered noisily as they waited for the town meeting that Paul had called at the last minute. This was the most exciting event that had ever come to the little village, and the residents were enjoying every moment. They cheered when Master James and his staff strode into the square.

"Give Master James your full attention," Paul requested. "And please, save your questions until the end of the meeting. Perhaps Master James will be good enough to entertain a few questions at that time."

"Indeed I shall," the engineer promised as he stood before the people. He paused to smile at the scores of children and young people present.

He raised his voice. "People of Hazah, thank you for the warm welcome that you extended to us today. We have enjoyed your hospitality already. And that was certainly an excellent feast that we enjoyed just moments ago.

"As each of you know, my men and I have been commissioned by His Majesty to build a castle for the protection of yourselves and your families. The building of a castle is no small undertaking. It will require dedication, hard work, and great sacrifice. Our adversary, Argamor, will oppose us in any way that he can. Many of you will have to set your own plans and goals aside for a time in order to accomplish this great task for your King, for in reality, the castle is for his honor and glory. Are you willing to undertake such a monumental task?"

A hearty chorus of "ayes" greeted him.

"Then let us begin," James said, pleased at the response. "But I warn you, once we get started, there is no turning back." He reached within his doublet and pulled out a rolled parchment. "Let us send a petition to Emmanuel seeking his help and guidance, for without his help, we can do nothing."

Raising his hand, he released the parchment, and the villagers watched as it shot from his hand to vanish over the top of the palisade in a streak of faint blue light. "I would encourage each of you to send petitions to His Majesty throughout this project that we might have his assistance every step of the way."

He paused. "My staff and I, with the assistance of some of your leaders, will in the next few days select a site for the building of the castle. We will try to plan it as close to the present location of your village as possible, and yet it must be a site that is easy to defend and that has a commanding view of the area.

"Once the site is chosen, we will design the castle itself. The main consideration is that it must be able to resist direct attacks by Argamor's forces and also withstand a siege.

"We will ask you to provide much of the labor. The project will require many workers, including quarrymen, stone masons, mortar mixers, diggers, carpenters, blacksmiths, and plumbers, just to name a few. There will be jobs for everyone. I have brought a staff of master craftsmen, and they will train you. These men will oversee your work and answer to me.

"You may be thinking, 'Master James, I have never built anything in my life—how can I build a castle?' Know this: every person here can serve Emmanuel in one way or another as we build together. We will train you."

Master James paused as he surveyed his audience. "I realize that most of you are already busy with your farms, your shops, your homes. As I said, this castle will require great sacrifice on your part. My men and I are making similar sacrifice; we have left our homes and families for a time to come and assist you in the building of your castle.

"Here's what King Emmanuel would ask of you: give one complete day each week to the construction of the castle. In addition, he would ask that you work until noon each day, and then utilize the rest of the day to work your own farms and businesses. In special situations or when special needs arise, you may request extra time to attend to your own affairs."

Master James smiled. "As you can see, this project will require sacrifice on each person's part. Your lives and your schedules are going to be drastically different until the building is complete. Again I ask, are you willing?"

The townspeople responded with a little less enthusiasm this time, but, one by one, nodded that they were ready to begin.

"I will do my best to keep you informed as the castle progresses. From time to time I will ask Paul to call a town meeting so that I may give you an update on the building, share any special problems or needs that arise, and also, seek your advice on various details.

"Thank you for gathering tonight. Now, are there any questions?"

"Sire, my fellow townspeople and I appreciate you and your staff coming to Hazah to help us with this castle project," Demas said, standing to his feet as he spoke. "We are grateful that His Majesty has received our petition and granted our request for a castle to protect our families from future assaults by Argamor and his followers. I have but one concern, sire." He paused.

Master James smiled patiently. "Name it, sir, and I will do my best to address it."

"Many of us have very busy lives and extremely demanding schedules," the merchant explained. "You have proposed that each of us will give a certain number of hours each week to the building project. Sire, what if some of us are simply not able to devote that much time?"

Master James was thoughtful, and he paused for a long moment before answering. "I'm sure that each of you will agree that the castle is to be the priority," he replied finally. "The castle is the work of His Majesty, and as we build it we serve him. As I said before, this project is no small undertaking. It will indeed require great dedication and great sacrifice."

"Perhaps some of us simply cannot make such a sacrifice, sire." Demas sat down.

Paul frowned as he listened to the exchange between his friend Demas and Master James, realizing for the first time that tremendous difficulties would lie ahead.

Chapter Four

"After considering several possibilities, my staff and I have settled on the exact location for the castle," Master James told the men assembled three days later on the hillside above the town, "subject to your approval, of course."

He swept his hand across the panorama before them. "We wanted a site as close as possible to the present site of the village," he explained, "to minimize the task of moving. The castle must also be close to the river, and it must be in a location that is easily defended."

He pointed. "That high outcropping of limestone which extends into the water is the ideal castle location for several reasons. It takes advantage of the natural defensive properties of the river, and at the same time allows for a good view of the adjacent land. We will locate the town at the foot of the outcropping where the castle site is accessible from land. This will necessitate moving the town about two furlongs."

He shrugged. "I would have preferred to leave the town as it is, but I'm sure you will see the reasons for the move."

"What if we were to build the castle right on the south edge of the town," Demas suggested, "so that all of our homes and shops could stay right where they are? Life would be much simpler that way."

The engineer shook his head. "That's not a good location."

"Why not, sire?" Demas demanded.

"The hillside where we stand right now is less than three hundred paces from the town," Master James explained. "In the event of an attack, archers could position themselves right where we stand now and effortlessly drop their arrows down into your town and pick off targets at will. Locating the town at the base of the outcropping will move it out of bow range."

Demas shrugged and nodded. "I see your point, sire."

Master James smiled. "The castle itself will come right out of the ground where we now stand," he said to the entire group.

"What do you mean, sire?" Matthew the baker wanted to know.

"Those boulders just above us on the hillside are the tip of a huge outcropping of sandstone. The stone used to build the castle walls will be quarried right out of the side of this mountain, right beneath our feet. Emmanuel has indeed smiled upon us in that we need not cart the stone any great distance."

"Father is furious," Rebecca reported to Phillip as soon as they were out of earshot of the village. The evening meal was over and the young couple was enjoying a stroll along the riverbank.

"Why?" Phillip asked.

"Well, Master James gave out the work assignments today, right?"

Phillip nodded. "I'm assigned to work with the carpenters."

"And I'm to help cook for Master James, his staff, and the other workers," Rebecca told him, "and also help carry water until the second well is finished. Anyway, Father was assigned to work as a quarryman."

Phillip grimaced. "That's hard work. Digging rock out of the side of a mountain is not an enjoyable way to spend your mornings."

Rebecca nodded. "That's the way Father figured it. He says that he and the others on the quarry crew will have to work twice as hard as any other workers."

"Master James plans to rotate some of the harder assignments just to keep things fair."

"I know. And I reminded Father of that fact. But he just complained that he got stuck in the least desirable position of all. He sees it as a deliberate move on Master James' part because he has voiced some objections to the castle project."

"Master James doesn't seem like the kind of man who would do that."

"You won't convince Father of that."

"Say, we're almost to the castle site," Phillip told Rebecca a moment later. "Let's go up on top of the outcropping and I'll show you the castle."

"The castle isn't there, silly," Rebecca responded with a giggle. "The builders haven't even started it yet."

"Aye, but Master James and his surveyors marked out the location with lime as they were planning it today," Phillip replied. "Come on, I can show you the basic layout so you can get an idea of how big the castle will be and where the various walls and towers will stand."

She followed him to the base of the outcropping.

"The diggers will dig the castle moat right across here," he told her, indicating with a sweep of his hand the very spot where they stood. "They'll build a ramp up to the edge of the moat, which will be the castle approach, with a drawbridge to allow access across the moat."

He started forward. "Come on, let's go up on top. I'll show you the rest of the layout of the castle."

Rebecca drew back. "We can't climb that."

"I'll help you," he reassured her. "It's not that hard."

Moments later they both stood atop the outcropping. "I've never been up here before," she ventured. "There's a good view of the river from here."

"I used to play up here when we were little," he told her. "The other boys and I would pretend that this was a castle and we would spend hours in battles attacking or defending the castle." He laughed. "Who would have ever guessed that one day a real castle would stand here?"

"You promised to show me the layout of the castle."

"That I shall, fair maiden, that I shall." He stepped closer to the northern edge of the outcropping and she followed him.

He indicated an area that had been marked on the ground with lines of dusty white powder. "Right here at the end of the drawbridge will be the main gate. You can see where a U-shaped tower will be built on each side of the gate, with the gatehouse directly above the gate.

"The wide line here is where the outer wall, called the outer curtain, will be. It's about a hundred yards along each of the four sides. Master James says that the outer curtain will be twenty-four feet high and nine feet thick. There will be four towers along each wall, but they'll be ten feet higher to provide a good view of the curtain on each side."

He walked toward the center of the castle layout. "This line marks the inner wall or the inner curtain, which will be about two hundred feet on a side. Those walls will be thirty-eight feet high and twelve feet thick. The towers will be fifty-two feet tall. The space between the outer curtain and the inner curtain is called the 'barbican,' or the 'outer ward,' and the courtyard within the inner curtain is called the 'bailey' or the 'inner ward.'"

Together Rebecca and Phillip stood where the bailey would one day be. "The great hall will be built against the south side of the inner curtain there, with the kitchen right beside it. Apartments for the servants and various castle residents will be built along the east wall, with barracks for a garrison of knights built across from it along the west wall."

"Why is the inner curtain going to be so much taller than the outer curtain?" the girl wanted to know.

"The increased height of the inner curtain will allow soldiers on top of it to fire over the outer curtain without hitting the soldiers guarding it. The tops of all the walls and towers on each curtain will be connected by walks that will allow knights to easily reach any part that might be under attack. When on top of the wall, knights will be protected by a narrow wall called a battlement that will be built along its outer edge."

Rebecca strolled casually across the castle site and Phillip followed her. "It's hard to imagine a castle standing right here, isn't it?" she said dreamily. "Imagine a band of dark knights trying to scale the castle walls while our knights are firing arrows and pouring boiling water on them." She turned to Phillip. "It gives you goose bumps just to think about it, doesn't it?"

Carefully they descended from the outcropping with Phillip helping Rebecca. "The town wall will start here at the corner of the castle and follow the outer perimeter of the town," Phillip told her. "Master James says that the town wall will be twenty feet high and six feet thick. The castle itself will require no special foundations because of its location on the limestone outcropping, but the workers will do some rough leveling where the walls will actually sit. The town wall, on the other hand, will not be all on rock, so the diggers will have to dig special foundation holes."

"This castle of ours is going to be a lot of work," the girl observed.

Phillip nodded. "Master James told us that the project would require great dedication and great sacrifice, but remember, the castle will offer great protection. When you think about what almost happened to Mira, all the work will be worth it. Remember, it is the work of Emmanuel, and he will provide the strength we need."

The work started in earnest the very next day. A crew of workmen began digging the moat across the landward side of the castle site while another group began digging the well for the castle. Still another group was put to work digging foundation holes for the town wall. Phillip was sent with the team of carpenters who joined the woodcutters in the forest for the arduous task of felling huge trees for lumber.

"We'll work with the lumberjacks just long enough to get a working supply of timber," one of Master James' staff told Phillip. "Once we have the lumber to begin working, we'll get to the real task of building."

Demas and a team of quarrymen trudged up the hillside above Hazah to begin the back-breaking task of excavating sandstone from the earth to provide the material to build the castle walls and towers. The foreman showed them how chisel away at the top of the rock structure in a horizontal line so that when freed the rock fell away in large sheets, which could then be broken up into smaller, more manageable blocks. After half an hour of strenuous labor, the quarry crew had filled just one oxcart with stone.

"This will take forever," one man complained.

"You'll get much faster as you learn how to do it," the foreman promised.

Demas put down his mallet and looked at his reddening hands. "I'm going to have so many blisters that I won't be able to hold the tools," he mourned.

"Your blisters will soon become calluses," he was told.

When the village gong was rung for the noon meal, the villagers were only too glad to stop work and come in for a much needed rest. Most were accustomed to hard work, but they were now doing tasks with which they were not familiar. Hungry and tired, they gathered in the village square.

Paul stood on a hay wagon and addressed them. "Well, my fellow villagers, the work has begun on the castle. As you can see, it will be a monumental task." He held up his hands and gave a rueful grin. "I had no idea that digging a well would be so much harder than my normal work."

The villagers laughed.

"Let's send a petition of thanksgiving to His Majesty, shall we?" Releasing the parchment in his hand, he watched as it disappeared over the treetops. Within moments, the workers were noisily enjoying bowls of venison stew and thick pieces of black bread being passed to them by a team of young maidens.

Rebecca managed to deliver Phillip's meal to him personally. "And how did your morning go?" she asked sweetly, though Phillip thought he detected a glimmer of mischief in her eyes.

He took the earthenware bowl she offered. "Felling trees is hard work! I'm ready for this stew."

She smiled and gave him a sly look. "I hope you're not too tired to take a walk with me this evening."

Phillip laughed. "If I am, Andrew will be glad to take you."

Her laughter was like the tinkle of a silver bell. "It's not your little brother I want to walk with, it's you." She moved away quickly.

"Thank you for the meal, fair maiden."

"Enjoy the food, brave sire," she called over her shoulder.

At that moment Andrew dropped to a seat beside him. "I helped the mortar makers dig sand for the mortar," he told his brother proudly. "I'm going to help again this afternoon."

Phillip reached out and affectionately tousled his brother's hair. "We're only working half a day today, so you have the rest of the afternoon off. Why not help me put up hay on Peter's farm?"

"Working on the castle is more fun," Andrew retorted. "Some of us are going to work all afternoon so that the castle gets finished quicker."

Without intending to, Phillip laughed out loud.

"What's so funny about that?" his brother demanded.

"Nothing at all. I'm just glad that you're so eager to help."

"Well, it's my castle, too."

"Actually, it's King Emmanuel's castle, but I'm thankful that we're allowed to help."

The boys' mother came along just then. "Did you save a seat for a poor working woman?" she asked, dropping to a seat on the ledge beside Andrew and then carefully placing her stew bowl in her lap.

"What have you been doing this morning, Ma?" Phillip asked. "Cooking?"

She drew herself up to her full height as if offended by the question. "I'll have you know, Master Phillip," she said haughtily, though both boys knew it was just an act, "that I have spent the morning hauling dirt and rubble from the moat."

"Ma," Phillip protested, "you're too old for that kind of work."

"Mind your tongue, lad," she replied sternly, though her eyes twinkled merrily, "or I'll get a hickory switch and thrash you right here in front of the whole village!"

Her son ducked his head meekly. "No offense intended, my lady."

She laughed. "And what crew did Master James place you on?"

"I'm a carpenter," he replied proudly. "Though today it seems I was a woodcutter, felling trees with the best of them."

"I'm so thankful we are to have a castle," she said thoughtfully, as she raised the bowl to her lips. "We need a place of safety from Argamor's attacks."

Just as most of the villagers were finishing their meal, Master James climbed atop the hay wagon. "Good people of Hazah," he said, speaking loudly enough for all to hear, "the work on the castle is off to a good start. I know that today many of you did jobs which you are not accustomed to, and many of you are tired and sore. In the next few days, as you learn and develop your skills, the work will go faster and the castle will begin to take shape right before your eyes.

"King Emmanuel has chosen a name for your castle; it is to be known as the Castle of Hope. He has also decreed a change of name for your village. No longer will it be known as Hazah, or 'sleeping.' From now on, your village will be called 'Mitspah,' which in the ancient language means 'watchful.' "

"Mitspah." The villagers looked at each other, each trying the new name out to see how it sounded.

"His Majesty would thank you for your hard work this morning. You are free to go to work on your own farms and shops this afternoon. My staff and I will begin the work of laying the outer curtain walls this afternoon. A few have asked if they may continue to work this afternoon, and the answer, of course, is yes. Any of you may help, or, if you wish, simply stop by to watch. We'll meet for our regular work assignments again at first light tomorrow morning."

"Where shall we meet if we wish to continue working?" the tailor called.

"Let's just meet here by the well," the engineer replied, "say, in half an hour?" He glanced over the crowd. "How many of you wish to work this afternoon? Would you mind raising your hands?" To his delight, more than half the villagers' hands immediately went up.

"Aye, excellent!" he exclaimed. "This is far more than I had anticipated. You have a will to work, and that is commendable. Why don't each of you report to your regular work stations? I think we will have enough on each crew to continue on with your regular tasks."

Demas stood to his feet, growling to Paul, "This slave driver seems to think that we have nothing better to do than toil away on his precious castle. I, for one, have work to do."

"I noticed that Phillip volunteered to work this afternoon," Paul replied.

"What concern is that of mine? Perhaps the lad has nothing better to do."

"I happen to know that he is doing the haying for Peter," the woodsman replied, "but he's setting that aside for the time to work on the castle. Demas, you can't rightly say that he is not a man of industry."

Demas walked away without answering.

"Timber!" A giant oak came crashing down, striking the earth with such force that Phillip could feel it shake the very ground upon which he stood. Phillip and two other men stepped over and began to trim off the branches with their axes. The ringing sound of axes biting into wood echoed throughout the forest as other woodsmen worked at felling other trees.

With a few energetic strokes of the axe Phillip cut through the first branch and stepped back to work on the next. Two young boys hurried forward to drag the branch to a nearby brush pile.

"Beware!" Just as the warning shout came to Phillip's ears he felt a tremendous blow to the calf of his leg, knocking him to the ground. He rose up on one hand and turned to see a huge gash in his leg. Blood was pouring profusely from the wound. Beside him on the ground was the shiny steel of an axe head.

"A thousand pardons, my lord!" The woodcutter, one of Master James' own crew, was beside him in an instant. "Are you all right? Let me see that leg."

The man drew back Phillip's legging and took a quick look at the gash. He sucked in his breath sharply. "It looks mighty bad, lad. We had better get that taken care of right away. Again, I ask your pardon. The axe head flew from my axe handle as I was felling a tree."

The foreman stepped over. "What happened?"

"The head flew from my axe and struck this man in the leg," the woodcutter replied meekly. "It's a serious wound, sire."

The foreman took a quick look. "Get him down to the village and have the surgeon fix him up."

"Aye, sire."

The foreman frowned at Phillip. "You'll do anything to get out of work, won't you?"

"Nay, sire," Phillip protested. "I want to be here!"

The man grinned. "I'm just teasing you, lad. The wound is bleeding quite a bit, but it's not as serious as it looks. We'll get you patched up and back to work in no time."

He turned to the woodcutter. "How did it happen?"

"Nay, I do not know, sire. I was felling a tree when the head flew from my axe and struck this unfortunate lad."

Another woodcutter retrieved the axe handle from the ground and handed it to the foreman. "Here's the handle, sire."

The foreman studied the broken handle. "It's been cut! This handle has been cut most of the way through!" He turned to the woodcutter. "Where did you get this axe?"

"From the regular tool supply cache, sire," the man replied nervously. "I used it all morning."

"Then someone cut it while you were eating the noon meal," the foreman said slowly. A dark look crossed his face. "That means that there is one among us who does not want the castle to be built. We have a saboteur in our midst."

Chapter Five

"You'll be good as new in no time," the surgeon promised Phillip as he finished bandaging the leg wound. The surgeon, an elderly man with disheveled white hair and a friendly smile, was one of Master James' own staff. "That was a serious cut and it bled quite a bit, but I don't think you did any permanent damage to the leg. Go easy next time, would you?"

"Can I go back to cutting wood?" Phillip queried eagerly.

"Great golden city, no, lad!" the man replied. "You should be thankful that you weren't crippled for life. You must stay off it for a few days; give the wound a chance to heal. Nay, there will be no woodcutting for you for the next little while."

"But we just started building the castle," Phillip protested. "I can't just lie around while everyone else is working."

The surgeon chuckled. "My, but you're an industrious one, are you not? Some folks I know would be glad to have an excuse to get out of work."

"This is His Majesty's castle we are building," Phillip said quietly. "By helping to build the castle I am serving King Emmanuel. That's why it's so important that I get back to work."

"You are right, lad, the castle is Emmanuel's work, and so in building the castle you are serving him. Never lose sight of that. But at the moment, you have been hindered by circumstances beyond your control, and King Emmanuel understands that. I'm afraid that you are out of commission for the next few days."

"But I can't just sit at home and do nothing," Phillip protested, "knowing that the work is going on without me."

"Suppose I have a couple of men carry you to the building site?" the old man asked kindly. "At least you'll be able to watch."

"I would be grateful, sire."

A short while later two workmen picked up the litter that the surgeon had prepared for his young patient. "Where to, young master? There are work projects going on all over the village."

"The one place that I most desire to be is perhaps the one place to which you cannot carry me."

"And where is that, pray tell?"

"The site of the castle itself," Phillip replied. "I don't suppose that you can carry me up on top of the outcropping."

"Are you challenging our strength and ability?" the man growled, though Phillip saw the twinkle in his eyes. "Come on, Mathias; let's show this young doubter what we're made of!"

Ten minutes later, Phillip was resting comfortably in the shade of an equipment shed that had been constructed where the inner castle curtain would one day stand. Fifteen paces away, a crew of stone masons was busily laying the first course of stone for the outer castle curtain wall. Master James himself was supervising. A few paces to Phillip's right, a workman was mixing mortar in a flat wooden box on the ground.

"You've got quite a bandage on your leg there," the man observed. "What happened?"

"I was felling wood when an axe head flew off and caught me

in the leg," Phillip explained.

The man grimaced. "Be thankful it didn't hit you in the head. Was it your axe or another's?"

"Another woodcutter's. The foreman says that the handle was deliberately cut to sabotage the work."

The mortar mixer let out a low whistle. "So one of Argamor's agents is in our midst, eh? It figures."

Phillip stared at him. "You think it was one of Argamor's men?"

"Who else? The castle was commissioned by His Majesty, so Argamor is opposed to its building." He looked thoughtful. "Does Master James know about the accident?"

"I don't think so."

"Then I'll tell him. We'll all have to be more careful."

The man stepped over and talked briefly with Master James. The engineer immediately came over to talk with Phillip.

"I'm sorry to hear of your accident, Phillip, though Mark tells me that it was not exactly an accident." He knelt beside Phillip. "Why don't you tell me what happened?"

Phillip repeated his story. When he had finished, Master James frowned. "Then it was an act of sabotage."

"Mark says that one of Argamor's agents is here somewhere," Phillip offered.

"Without a doubt," the man replied, "though that was to be expected. I would be surprised if there is not more than one. I just didn't expect them to move so quickly." He laid a hand on Phillip's knee. "Thank you for telling me what you know. My staff and I will have to decide upon a course of action to protect the castle and the workers." He hurried back to his work.

Mark resumed the mixing of the mortar. Noticing Phillip's interest in the building of the castle walls, he began to explain their construction. "The inner and outer faces of each wall are being constructed first," he said. "The stones will be fitted and then mortared in horizontal rows known as courses. When a height of three or four feet is reached, the space between these two narrow walls will be completely filled with rubble."

"Rubble?"

"A mixture of stones and mortar. As we build, master masons will continually check both the horizontal and vertical accuracy of the walls."

Phillip studied the mixture in the mortar box. "What's in the mortar?"

"A mixture of water, sand, and lime."

Phillip watched in silence as the castle curtain slowly took shape before his eyes. The villagers who were serving as assistants hauled stone up from the carts below using a system of ropes and pulleys attached to beams suspended out over the side of the precipice. They dumped the stone in neat piles close to the location for the wall. Stone masons then placed each stone in course and mortared it in place with quick movements of their trowels. Young boys from the village served as mortar carriers and made sure that each stone mason was kept supplied with plenty of mortar. There were so many workers and so much activity that the building of the wall reminded Phillip of the frenetic activity usually found around an ant hill.

Before the afternoon was finished, the outer face of the outer curtain on the north side was nearly two feet high and the inner face had two complete courses of stone laid. Finally, Master James clanged two iron tools together to get the attention of the workers. "You've done a good day's work and we've made an excellent start. Clean your tools and then go home and get some rest. Spend some time with your children. Tomorrow we'll get a fresh start on the castle."

The mortar mixer gave a low grunt of satisfaction. "I'm

ready for a break," he said as he began to scrape the loose mortar from the wooden box. "This has been a long day and I'm tired and hungry." He grinned suddenly. "But we did make an excellent start on the outer curtain, didn't we?"

Phillip nodded. "It's finally starting to take shape."

The man glanced at Phillip's bandages. "How's the leg?"

"It hurts a bit," Phillip admitted, "but I'm all right."

"As soon as I get my tools put away I'll get a friend to help me carry you back to the village."

"I would be grateful, sire."

The next morning after a simple breakfast of gruel and boiled gourds Phillip fashioned a makeshift crutch from a sturdy branch with a fork at one end. Using a borrowed bow saw he shortened the forked branches and then smoothed them as best he could. He wrapped an old piece of sacking around the forked end for padding. Andrew came in just he was finishing. "What are you making?"

"A crutch," his brother replied. "I'm not going to have people carrying me around; I'll get around on my own."

He stood to his feet, placed the padded end of the crutch under his armpit, then took a tentative step or two. "Just a bit too long," he decided. "I'll shorten it just a bit and then I'll be walking as usual."

Twenty minutes later he gave a sigh of relief as he stepped up on top of the castle site. As he sank to a seat beside the equipment shed he noticed that the stone masons and other workers were all clustered together in an animated discussion, and he sensed that something was amiss. Spotting him, Mark hurried over toward him. "How's the leg this morning?"

"All right, but what's happened?" Phillip asked. "Something's wrong; I can tell."

"The curtain wall has been damaged," Mark told him soberly. "A number of the stones have been deliberately knocked out of their courses."

"Deliberately?"

"It was the work of a saboteur," the man replied, "perhaps the one who cut the axe handle yesterday."

"How much of the wall was destroyed?" Phillip inquired.

"That's what is odd about it. Whoever did the damage did not destroy the entire wall; they just knocked down ten yards or so of the outer course of the wall and then a little further down, three or four yards of the inside course. The damage that was done took less than a minute to accomplish. Why did the saboteur not take just a few more minutes and destroy the entire wall? It doesn't make sense."

Phillip sighed. "But why would anyone want to hinder the work of building the Castle of Hope?"

"The saboteur, whoever he or she is, is an agent of Argamor. The Castle of Hope was commissioned by King Emmanuel, so Argamor is bent on hindering the work of building it."

"But then why did not this saboteur destroy the entire length of wall? Why stop after just a minute or two of destruction?"

Mark frowned. "Aye, that's what I'd like to know. It's almost as if this person is trying to send us a message, rather than just outright destroy our work."

"What kind of message?"

The man shrugged. "A message of fear, perhaps. Or discouragement. It's as if he wants to let us know that he can destroy anything we build. Perhaps he wants us to feel that we must always be looking over our shoulder."

"Well, he won't stop the work on the castle," Phillip said with determination.

"Nay, he won't," Mark agreed. "It will be but the work of an hour or two to rebuild the damaged section of the wall, and Master James will post a guard tonight, I'm sure."

Master James called the workers together and Phillip joined them.

"As we all know," the engineer said, "the damage to the curtain wall is the work of a saboteur, perhaps the same one who damaged the axe yesterday resulting in the injury to our young friend Phillip. At any rate, this evil deed was the work of an agent of Argamor, and done at his direction.

"We will repair the damage and continue building. This act of sabotage will not hinder the building of the Castle of Hope. But this evil saboteur is still among us, and we must be alert and watchful at all times until he is caught. We will post a guard at each of the worksites, but I will ask each of you to be alert and watchful. Report to me directly if you see anything suspicious."

He smiled. "Are you ready for another productive day in the construction in the Castle of Hope? Aye, then let's go to work!"

As the stone masons began their work Phillip took a seat beside the shed. His leg wound was throbbing just a bit and he felt light-headed. Moments later, Master James came over and spoke to him. "Good morning, Phillip, and how's that leg of yours?"

"It's all right, sire. It hurts a bit, but give me a few days and I'll be back to normal. I can't wait to get back to work on the castle."

The man smiled. "I appreciate your spirit. By the way, what work crew did I place you on?"

"I'm with the carpenters, sire, though yesterday I was cutting timber with the woodcutting crew when the accident happened."

"The townspeople tell me that you're an expert archer—is that correct?"

"Aye, well, whoever said that may have stretched things a bit, but I am handy with a longbow, sire. My father was an expert archer, and he trained me."

"Are you a huntsman?"

"Aye, sire, I love to hunt."

"How plentiful is the game in this region?"

"The game abounds here. Harts, roebuck, rabbits, grouse and pheasant—they're everywhere! Why do you ask, sire?"

Master James sighed. "There are a few bowmen on my staff whom I have given the task of keeping venison on our tables, but so far they are not producing much of anything." Thoughtfully, he studied Phillip for a moment. "How would you like to change assignments and be placed on a different work crew?"

"I'll do anything to help, sire. What would you have me do?"

"Rest that leg for a few more days. Make sure that it is healed properly. And then, when you are ready, I would like for you to become my master hunter. Spend a few days with my men and teach them how to hunt this region. After that, you are on your own. Your responsibility will be to keep venison on our tables. I'll even give you a horse so that you can cover more range and avoid overhunting the area close to the village. Can you handle that?"

"Aye, sire!" the young man responded with enthusiasm. "There is almost nothing that I would enjoy more." A disturbing thought crossed his mind. "But, sire, if I'm to hunt for you, I won't have time to help build the castle."

"A multitude of different tasks are involved in the building of a castle," the man answered thoughtfully, "and His Majesty has equipped various people with different skills and abilities. In His Majesty's service, each task is just as important as any other. The lass who cleans up after the morning meal is just as important to Emmanuel as the master mason who builds the castle wall.

"In providing meat for the workers who are building the Castle of Hope, you are actually building the Castle of Hope. His Majesty has given you a skill that you may use to great advantage in his service, and I am simply making use of the skill he has given you. Are you willing to hunt for me?"

"Aye, that I am, sire. Thank you for trusting me with this duty."

"Don't get too eager to start," Master James said with a smile. "Rest a few days and allow that wound to heal properly. I don't want you in the forests until you show me that the leg is healed. Understand?"

Phillip nodded. "I thank you, sire."

"Master James wants you to do what?" Demas was nearly shouting. Phillip and Rebecca had just returned from their evening stroll and the girl had told her father about Phillip's new assignment.

"He wants me to hunt for the village and for his work crews," the youth replied.

"I thought you were assigned to work with the carpenters," Demas said flatly. "How will you do both?"

"Master James took me off the carpenter crew and gave me this new assignment. I'm to start hunting as soon as my leg heals."

"Well, how do you like that?" Demas said bitterly. "I'm breaking my back splitting rocks all day for this castle project, and you're going to spend your days loafing in the forests."

Without thinking, Rebecca blurted, "Master James is going to give Phillip a horse, Father, so that he can range farther from the village on his hunts."

Demas was beside himself with rage. "A horse? The man is going to give you a horse? All of my life I have wanted a horse, worked day and night to buy one, and still do not have one. And this...this Master James gives you an assignment where you don't even have to work, and then he gives you a horse!"

Jealousy flooded the man's soul, raging in his heart and poisoning his mind until he was so furious he was trembling. "Get out of my house," he growled. "Get out now, and never return."

"But, sire..."

"You are never to see my daughter again, do you hear me? Never! Don't ever let me catch you near her again!"

"But, Father," Rebecca pleaded, "have you already forgotten? Phillip is the one who saved Mira's life! How can you reject him from our house?"

Demas turned on his daughter in fury. "Silence, daughter, or you'll wish you had never been born!"

Phillip bowed his head and hobbled dejectedly from the room as Rebecca began to weep.

Chapter Six

Longbow in hand, Phillip crept silently up the steep forest trail. The forest was dark and shadowy here, and he leaned forward, studying the ground for hoof prints of the hart he had been tracking. When he first spotted it he had been downwind of the animal and nearly two hundred paces away, but somehow the hart had sensed his presence and bounded away before the young huntsman could move closer or draw an arrow from his quiver.

The hart was huge, with an impressive spread of antlers, and Phillip had decided that he would have to take this magnificent trophy if it took all day to bring him down. He had been tracking the animal for more than an hour now and estimated that he had hiked more than thirty furlongs. But his quarry was now doubling back toward Mitspah, and he was slowing down and showing signs of tiring, so Phillip stayed with him. It would only be a matter of time before he had the magnificent animal within bow range.

He paused beside a huge granite boulder and took a long drink from his water flask. His mind replayed the events of the last few days. He had been the master hunter for a fortnight now, and in those fourteen days of hunting had managed to bring in two or more sizable deer each day, as well as numerous rabbits and game birds. As a result of the bountiful hunting, food had been plentiful at the village tables. Master James and the villagers had been delighted with his work. On one particularly good day he had actually brought in five deer. The harts and roebucks were so plentiful in the region that he had developed the habit of passing by the smaller, younger deer, knowing that he would soon come upon larger, more mature animals.

His reputation had grown in the village. Each time he returned from a hunt, villagers young and old thronged about his horse, eager to see what he had bagged that day and begging for stories of the day's hunt. It seemed as if they were more interested in his hunting than in the progress being made in the building of the Castle of Hope.

He sighed. As his popularity had grown, Rebecca's father's hatred for him had seemed to grow in direct proportion. Demas' jealousy had reached the point where he would turn and walk the other way if he even saw Phillip approaching. Needless to say, Phillip had been allowed no time with Rebecca.

"I miss you, my love," he said aloud, closing the flask and slinging it over his shoulder. "I can't live without you! But how do I get your stubborn father to change his mind?"

He started up the trail. His keen eyes still scoured the ground for the hart's tracks, but his mind was far away. "We haven't had a sunset walk in more than a fortnight, my love," he said with a quiet sigh. "Do you even know how much I miss you?"

His thoughts turned to the castle. The work was progressing rapidly; in fact, the north outer curtain wall was now fifteen feet high, and the east and west walls were already nearly six feet high. Work had started on the northeast and northwest towers. The well diggers had reached a depth of forty-four feet, and Master James estimated that they had less than forty feet more to go before they struck water. The Castle of Hope was indeed taking shape, and Phillip loved to go each evening after the hunt and view the day's progress.

"Oh, but how I miss the evening walks with Rebecca," he whispered aloud.

Sensing movement, he slowly turned his head. The hart was standing in a thicket less than thirty paces away! Phillip held his breath. His quarry was upwind and facing directly away from him. Scarcely daring to breathe, he slipped an arrow onto the bowstring and pulled back to full draw.

Twang! The arrow sped from the string to strike the huge deer just behind the shoulder. The animal dropped without a sound. Phillip ran forward to ascertain that the deer was truly dead and then pulled the arrow from the carcass. "My best kill yet!" he exulted. He reached out and gently touched the hart. The animal's fur had an unusual color and sheen to it, almost as if it were spun from gold. "A golden hart," he said softly. He struggled to drag the heavy body from the thicket and then went in search of his horse.

Half an hour later he rode back into the clearing to retrieve the carcass. "You're going to have quite a load to carry back to the village," he told Tabitha, the big, sturdy mare given him by Master James. "This is by far the largest hart I have taken yet!"

He reined to a stop and looked about in bewilderment. The carcass was gone. Puzzled, he rode forward. The golden hart was nowhere to be seen. Suddenly Tabitha snorted and side-stepped, shying from the trail as if in fear.

"Whoa, Tabitha! Easy, girl!"

Phillip started to dismount, but the big horse reared up slightly and then continued to side-step, whinnying and snorting as if highly distressed. Leaning low in the saddle, the young huntsman studied the ground beneath the oak tree where he had left the carcass of the golden hart. He sucked in his breath sharply. Cat tracks! A cougar had stolen his best kill!

Knowing that it was best not to tangle with the cougar, Phillip wheeled Tabitha around and galloped from the area. Anger welled in his heart toward the huge cat. "The biggest hart I've ever taken, and that wretched cougar has to steal it from me!" he raged aloud.

He glanced toward the sky, checking the position of the sun. "Oh, well, there's still another hour to hunt. Perhaps I can take another." A rabbit bounded across the trail just then, and within moments was safely tucked away in Phillip's game bag.

An hour later, Phillip rode toward home. A small doe lay behind his saddle. "I'd still rather have the huge buck," he told Tabitha, "but at least we're not going back empty-handed. And I did get two harts this morning."

Three or four furlongs from the village he slowed Tabitha to a walk. He had spotted the figure of a woman sitting on a fallen log beside the trail. She was watching him, and obviously waiting for him. His heart leaped. Rebecca! Urging the mare to a gallop, he raced to meet her.

He swung from the saddle and she stood with a smile of welcome. "Phillip!"

"Rebecca, what are you doing out here?"

"Mother sent me to gather herbs," she said sweetly, "and I figured that this would be the best place to search for them since this is the time when you usually return from the hunt." She gave him a sly look. "I watched you leave, so I knew you came this way."

He laughed, delighted to be in her presence once again. "Darling, you cannot know how I have missed you!"

"And I you," she whispered softly. "Oh, Phillip, what are we going to do? Father is unyielding."

"First of all," he chided gently, "we're going to stop meeting like this. This is a bit deceitful, you know."

"I had to see you," she pouted. "I had to know whether or not you still loved me."

Phillip's heart ached. "I always will," he said quietly. "That will never change."

She raised her eyes to him, and he saw that they were filled with tears. "Why can't we meet here every day or two, my love? Father has no right to keep us apart."

He sighed. "You don't know how much I would want that. But your father is the authority in your life, and at this point in your life you must obey him. I also have to respect his decision."

"Do you know how hard it is to go without seeing you, my love? I can hardly bear it. I see you about the village and watch you from a distance, but I long to talk with you, to be close to you."

His heart ached. "I feel the same things, my love, but we must be patient. Someday your father will change his mind, and then we can be with each other again."

"That will never happen," she sobbed.

"All things are possible," he replied quietly.

Rebecca dried her eyes and attempted a smile. "I'm sorry to be so weepy. It's just that I miss you so much, Phillip. If Father won't let us see each other, what hope is there that he'll let us get married?" She stopped, suddenly embarrassed. "I keep talking about it, but you haven't even asked me yet."

"Someday I will, my love. Someday soon."

Still embarrassed, she turned away from him, and then noticed the doe behind the saddle. "You got another hart. You're quite the hunter, you know. The entire village talks about you. I have heard that Master James has said that you are the best huntsman he has ever seen."

Phillip smiled modestly. "I enjoy the assignment that he gave me. I love hunting." His eyes lit up. "You should have seen the hart that I lost today."

"Lost?" Rebecca looked puzzled.

"It was by far the biggest hart that I have ever seen," he said enthusiastically, "with a pelt that looked as if it were fashioned from spun gold. I tracked him for over an hour and then finally got close enough to drop him."

"Did you?"

"Aye, I dropped him with one shot. I removed my arrow from the carcass and then trekked back to get Tabitha. When I returned, the carcass was gone."

"What happened?" she asked.

"I'm not sure. I found cougar tracks all over the area when I returned, but I didn't see signs that the cougar had dragged the hart away. But with the cougar in the area, I didn't stay around to figure it out. Tabitha and I got out of there. You should have seen the hart, Rebecca. It was huge!"

He glanced at the sun and then playfully gave her a stern look. "You had better get back home, love. Your mother is awaiting those herbs."

She sighed. "Will I see you again tomorrow?"

He frowned. "My love, we must wait. We cannot go against your father's wishes."

"But Phillip, suppose he never changes his mind? Must we wait forever?"

"I hope not, my love." He smiled sadly as he mounted Tabitha. "I'm going to talk with Paul. He and your father have been friends since childhood—perhaps he can advise me as to what to do to win your father over."

He gave her a tender look and then rode away.

Paul and Phillip sat on the back of an oxcart parked on the hillside above the village. Behind them was the newly-dug rock quarry, a wide, deep gash in the earth, extending across the side of the hill for nearly a hundred paces. In places, the quarry was nearly twenty feet deep. After several moments of silence, Paul spoke. "I don't know what to tell you, Phillip. Demas can be a very stubborn man. Once he makes up his mind, it can be nearly impossible to get him to change it."

"But he's forbidden Rebecca and me to even see each other," the young huntsman protested. "What are we to do? He doesn't even allow us to talk with each other. I love her, Paul, and I believe that she loves me. We're both having a hard time with this. And there's no reason for the separation."

"Demas can be extremely jealous at times," Paul replied. "I've known him since he was a young boy, and he's always been that way."

"You know what caused it, don't you, sire?"

Paul nodded. "Aye. You were given a work assignment that you absolutely love while he has an assignment that he detests. On top of that, you were given a horse, which is something he has always wanted. He simply doesn't know how to deal with this. He's striking out at you in the only way he knows."

"By striking out at me he's hurting his own daughter."

Paul nodded. "I know, and I'm sure that he knows. But he's too proud and too vengeful to reconsider."

"Can you talk with him, sire? I'm begging you!"

"I don't know that it will do any good, Phillip, but I can certainly try. But don't expect any change. Demas can be a very stubborn and obstinate man, as we both know. He's never been fond of you, and now with the irritations of the job assignments and the horse, he's furious with you. I'm sorry, son, but that's the way it is."

Phillip sighed. "I'm the one who saved Mira from the invaders!"

Paul nodded. "I know. And one would think that Demas would be forever grateful to you for that very reason. But apparently his jealousy outweighs any sense of gratitude that he might feel toward you."

"What am I to do?"

The man shook his head. "I don't know. All I can tell you to do is wait. Wait and hope for a miracle."

"Should Rebecca and I try to see each other on the sly?"

"If Demas found out—and he would find out eventually, for one can't keep secrets in a small village—that would only make things worse. For you, and especially for her. It's best to wait and see what develops."

"It's so hard to wait, sire. We both feel as if we can't live without each other."

Paul smiled. "I understand."

Several days later, Phillip rode in from the hunt just as the quarrymen were finishing work. It was the one day of the week when the villagers were required to give a full day's labor, and the men were exhausted. Phillip reined to the left side of the road to pass the workmen and realized that the nearest quarryman was Demas. In a sudden impulse of boldness, he dismounted and confronted the man.

"Sire, I must talk with you."

Demas eyed him coldly. "I have nothing to say to you, lad, and you cannot possibly have anything to say of interest to me.

Go about your business."

"Sire, you must reconsider! I implore you, allow me to see your daughter once again."

"I wouldn't think of it. Now leave me alone and let me be about my business. I've had a hard day and I have no time for this foolishness."

Phillip was desperate. "Sire, remember, I'm the one who saved Mira from the dark knights when they attacked the village! Do you not remember? Does that not count for anything?"

Demas stepped around him without answering. Angrily, he walked toward Distinction River, heading directly away from the village.

The north outer curtain wall of the Castle of Hope was nearly finished. Nine feet thick, it rose twenty-two feet in the air and stretched for three hundred feet across the top of the limestone outcropping. The castle was starting to take on a formidable appearance. As the walls increased in height, a temporary framework, or scaffolding, had been erected to support the workers and materials. The poles were lashed together and fastened to the walls by horizontal logs inserted into special holes in the walls. Planks were nailed to the scaffolding, and it was upon these planks that the stone masons worked as they built the wall ever higher.

"Just a few more courses of stone and the wall will be the prescribed height of twenty-four feet," the master stone mason told Master James as they started work one morning. "The north curtain is almost finished, except for the towers and gatehouses."

"The work has progressed quickly," Master James remarked.

"The Castle of Hope is rapidly taking shape."

"Good morning, Master James." Three stone masons carrying tools passed them and started up the inclined ramp that led to the top of the scaffolding.

"Good morning, men."

Just as the men reached the top of the wall, the scaffolding gave way with a loud cracking sound. Timbers, stones, and tools came crashing down as a number of workmen tumbled to the ground.

Two of the workmen were pinned to the ground by the falling timbers. Another man, struck by falling tools, was lying upon the ground, obviously in pain. After a moment of stunned silence, Master James ran forward. Several workmen joined him in lifting the timbers of the scaffolding to free the injured men.

"Get the surgeon," Master James instructed a worker. "This man's leg is obviously broken."

When the injured men had been cared for, Master James and the workers began to examine the fallen structure. "What could have caused the collapse?" the master engineer wondered aloud.

"Here's a possible cause, sire," a stone mason offered. "Some of the lashings have been untied."

"When were they checked last?" Master James inquired.

"Joshua and I personally checked them yesterday evening," a worker reported, "just as the crew was finishing the shift. They were tight, sire, every one of them."

"Aye, we double-checked each of them," Joshua agreed. "They were tight, sire."

Master James' jaw tightened. "Then the damage to the scaffolding was done deliberately, and it must have been done some time last evening or during the night. The saboteur is at work again. We must find and stop him before he kills some of you."

Chapter Seven

Two stone masons' assistants stood nervously before Master James. "Sire, we must report what happened last evening. It's possible that we saw the saboteur."

Instantly the boys had Master James' attention. "Tell me what you saw," he urged.

"Last evening after we finished work," one of the boys began, "Thomas and I were walking back toward the village when we turned for a look at the north curtain. I spotted a man on the scaffold and pointed him out to Thomas. We wondered who he was and what he was doing, but didn't think any more of it at the time. This morning when the scaffold collapsed, we both realized that the man on the scaffold must have been the saboteur."

Master James leaned forward eagerly. "Did you see who it was? Did you get a look at his face?"

The boys both shook their heads. "We were too far away for that, sire, but we could see that he was a small man." They hesitated and looked at each other for reassurance. "Sire, we both think that the saboteur was Demas."

"Demas." Master James paused. "Are you certain?"

"Nay, sire, but we could clearly see that the man on the

scaffold had a small, slender build. We were too far away to be sure, but we think it was Demas."

Master James called a town meeting that evening just before sunset. "I wish to thank each of you for your hard work on the Castle of Hope," he began. "This is a huge project, but with all of us working together, we are making excellent progress. Always remember that the work is for the honor and glory of His Majesty, King Emmanuel.

"As you have heard, there was another act of sabotage on the north curtain wall. The scaffold collapsed under the workmen. Two of our number were seriously injured, but thankfully, most of the workmen escaped injury."

He paused and looked over the villagers. "We are presently working on the problem. As a matter of fact, we now believe that we may have information as to the identity of the saboteur."

Instantly, the town square buzzed with excitement.

"Two of the masonry assistants saw a man on the scaffold just after the work crew left, and we have reason to believe that this man may have been the saboteur."

Master James then went on to discuss plans for the castle construction and gave further instructions for the work that would be involved. As he dismissed the assembly, he asked the quarry crew to remain behind. The men gathered around him.

"Demas," the master engineer said, "two witnesses think that they saw you on the scaffolding at the time of the sabotage."

Demas was belligerent. "You suspect me?"

"What do you have to say, sire?"

"You have to be insane!" Demas said hotly. "I'm not your saboteur!"

"Can you tell me where you were just after work was halted for the day?"

Indignant, Demas refused to answer.

"Did you or did you not untie the lashings on the scaffolding on the north curtain wall of the castle, causing it to collapse this morning and bring injury to the workmen?"

"I did not!" Demas replied furiously. "This is ridiculous!"

Master James looked across the group of men. "Can any of you quarrymen vouch for this man's whereabouts at the time in question?" he asked. "It would have been just after the work on the castle wall was halted for the night."

"Demas left when we did," one quarry worker volunteered. "We didn't see what he did then."

Phillip was passing by and had overheard part of the conversation. *That's when I talked with Demas,* he realized. *He couldn't have been the one whom they saw on the scaffold!*

"Demas, this is a very serious charge," Master James said sternly. "Do you have any proof of your whereabouts at the time in question?"

"I left the quarry with the other workers," Demas growled. "The man on the scaffold wasn't me. I haven't been to the castle site since this wretched project began."

"Can you prove your claims?"

"Nay," the accused man growled. "You'll have to take my word for it."

Master James frowned. "This is a very serious charge against you, Demas, and—"

Phillip stepped closer. "The man on the scaffold wasn't Demas!"

Master James looked at him in surprise. "Phillip! What do you know of this?"

"Yesterday evening I was returning from the hunt just as the quarry workers were leaving the quarry site," the young hunts-man explained. "It was at that same time the work crew were leaving the castle site, for I remember looking up at the castle wall and seeing them in the distance as I rode in."

"How do you know that the man on the scaffold was not Demas?"

"I talked with him for a couple of moments below the quarry. When we parted, Demas walked down to the river, heading north, away from town. I mounted Tabitha and sat thinking for several minutes. Demas could not have gone to the castle site without me seeing him, unless he swam the river to do it."

A murmur of excitement swept across the group.

Master James sighed. "Demas, I owe you an apology, and I ask for your forgiveness and understanding. On numerous occasions you have voiced opposition to the building of the Castle of Hope, and you have voiced your discontent with your work assignment. When the report came of a man matching your description, it was only natural to think the worst, and I ask your forgiveness for the mistake."

He looked across the group of quarrymen. "Our meeting is adjourned."

Phillip and Andrew were walking home with their mother when Phillip felt a hand on his arm. He turned to see Demas standing nervously beside him. "I need to talk with you, lad."

Phillip nodded and motioned for his mother and brother to continue without him.

"I—I wish to thank you, lad, for speaking up as you did. You must have been tempted to keep silent after the way I've treated you of late." He looked at the ground and then back up at Phillip. "I'm asking for your forgiveness, Phillip."

"You have it, sire," Phillip said quietly.

The man hesitated, and Phillip sensed that the words were difficult. "I'm a very selfish person, as you know, and sometimes my selfishness gets the best of me. These last two or three weeks have been very hard for me, lad. I hate the quarry work with a passion, while you love the work assignment that was given to you. For years I have waited to replace my little donkey with a horse, but I have been unable to. When Master James gave you a horse, well, something fell apart inside me, and I couldn't take it any longer. I lashed out at you in the only way that I could—by taking Rebecca from you."

He sighed and fell silent for a moment. "In trying to hurt you, I am hurting my daughter, and I just can't do that anymore. Tonight, when you stood up for me, I realized what a fool I have been in trying to keep you two apart."

Demas bowed his head in humility. "I'd like to ask you to come by the house and see my daughter, if you would."

Phillip's heart leaped for joy.

The western sky was ablaze with color as the sun set over the kingdom of Terrestria. Phillip and Rebecca walked slowly along the river's edge. Rebecca let out a long sigh of contentment. "It's been so long, my love, since we walked here. Sometimes I wondered if we would ever walk together again."

He sighed with contentment. "As did I," he replied softly. "To be honest, I often despaired of ever taking a walk like this again."

He looked at her. "What did your father tell you?"

"Just that he was sorry for refusing to let us see each other, and that he had given you permission to see me again."

"Anything else?"

She blushed. "He also said that he thought you would make an excellent son-in-law."

"Today is the last day in the quarry for half of the crew," the quarry foreman told his workers the next day as they were preparing to start work. "Tomorrow half of you will rotate out to a new work assignment, while the remaining half will stay one more day to help train the new crew. The next day the rest of you will rotate out."

"This doesn't come a moment too soon," Demas growled, and the other men laughed, knowing how much he despised the quarry. "Please tell me that I'm on the list for the first rotation."

The foreman consulted a parchment. "I'm sorry, Demas, but you're on the second. You have two more days with me, my friend."

Demas shrugged. "I suspected as much."

"What about us?" asked one of the young boys on the crew.

The man glanced across the group of youth who clustered around him. "Half of you will rotate to another assignment also," he told them. "I must say that you young men have done a good job. We're thankful for your help."

An hour later, several men atop an eight-foot scaffolding worked on a sheer wall of sandstone nearly thirty feet high. Using hammers and hand drills, they were attempting to cut a small section free when the entire wall began to move. "Jump clear!" the foreman shouted. Dropping their tools, the workmen leaped from the scaffold and scrambled to safety.

With a thunderous roar, countless tons of rock tumbled down, completely burying the scaffold. A cloud of dust filled the air.

"Is everyone all right?" the foreman asked loudly, dusting himself off as he hurried forward.

"We're all here," a workman answered a moment later.

"Are the boys all right?"

"They're all here and accounted for," the same man replied, "though I dare say the scaffolding is destroyed."

"Our tools are buried with it," said another.

"It seemed as if the entire mountain was coming down on us," remarked a third.

"We can be thankful that none of us were hurt," the foreman told them. He glanced again at the group of boys as if to reassure himself that they had not been injured.

The workers stood at the base of the rockslide staring up at the spot where they had been laboring just moments before. "That was a little too close."

The foreman shrugged. "I'm sorry to have placed you men in jeopardy. I've never seen anything like this. A moment or two ago that wall seemed solid. There must have been a fault that I didn't see—I certainly didn't expect it to break free like that."

Demas pointed. "Look. What is that?"

The other men gazed at the rockslide where he pointed. "What are you talking about, Demas?"

"Right there in the wall, about five or six feet above the rock pile. Don't you see it? It looks like gold!"

"I don't see anything unusual," one man replied.

"Nor I," said another.

"There's something shiny up there, and whether or not it's gold, I'm going to find out what it is," Demas retorted sharply. Glancing around, he spotted a hammer and small chisel lying nearby. Retrieving the tools, he cautiously climbed the mound of fallen rock.

"Be careful, Demas," the foreman called. "The slide could still be loose. Boys, move back!" The youth retreated obediently.

"Demas has abandoned quarry work and gone to mining," a workman joked, and the others laughed.

"What is it?" the men called as Demas neared the spot, which was about fifteen feet above the ground.

"I don't know yet," the man replied, placing the tip of the chisel to one side of the shiny object. He gave a sharp tap with the hammer. Instantly the sandstone around the object disintegrated, expelling the object from the rock as if the mountain had given birth. Dropping the chisel, Demas deftly caught the object as it fell.

"What is it?"

Demas was speechless. He slowly backed down the rocky slope, holding the glittering object in both hands. "It's a lamp," he said at last, whispering in awe. "A lamp made of solid gold!"

At that moment an old man arrayed in a flowing robe stepped forward and grabbed Demas by the arm, gripping him so hard that the other man winced in pain. "It's one of the golden lamps," he said hoarsely. "Get rid of it, my friend! Free yourself from the golden lamp before it exerts its power upon you."

Demas and the other quarrymen stared at the old man. "Who are you," Demas demanded, "and where did you come from?"

"My name is not important, nor is the place from whence I came," the old man replied. "It is my words that matter. Make haste, before it is too late! Hurl the lamp from you as far as you possibly can!"

Chapter Eight

"Get rid of the lamp," the old man urged again. His eyes were wide with fear and he moved away from Demas as if the proximity of the lamp might bring him harm. "Rid yourself of that wretched object, my friend, before it destroys you!"

"What are you talking about?" Demas replied incredulously. "If this is gold it will buy me a horse! It will buy me ten horses!"

"One horse or ten, it matters not," the old man replied. "Ten horses would not be worth the trouble that lamp can bring. Better to free yourself from the lamp now, while you still can."

The boys on the crew watched in astonishment. Several moved closer for a better look at the lamp, but the foreman spread his arms wide and held them back.

Demas stared at the lamp, completely mesmerized by its beauty. The other quarrymen gathered around him. "It is gold," one said in awe. "It's worth a fortune!"

"Hurl it from you! Destroy it before it destroys you!" Shaking with fear, the old man crept further away.

"Old man," the foreman said, "Come here. Why are you so fearful? Why do you insist that Demas must destroy the lamp?"

Cautiously, the old man crept closer, but he refused to get too close. "There is an ancient legend," he said in a trembling voice. "The legend holds that many eons ago, shortly after King Emmanuel created Terrestria, forty golden lamps were forged deep within the mountains by an evil one. The lamps were created to lead men astray."

The mysterious visitor glanced nervously around. The quarrymen were gathered close, leaning forward and hanging on his every word. "If the legend is true, the lamps bring prosperity to those who find them."

"Did you hear that, Demas?" a worker said, clapping Demas on the back. "Prosperous times are ahead for you."

Demas grinned.

"The lamp has already brought good fortune to us," a workman remarked. "The rockslide may have destroyed our scaffolding, but it has broken more rock than we could have broken in three weeks!"

"Do not jest about the matter," the old man warned. He turned to Demas. "Nor should you rejoice in your good fortune, for there is more to the legend."

Demas grew somber. "What do you mean?"

"The power of the lamp can be used for good or for evil," the old man replied in a dark tone. "Should you choose to use the lamp for good, it will become a tremendous blessing to you and to those around you. But should you choose to use it for evil, the lamp will become a curse to you, as well as to those around you."

Demas shrugged. "Then I will choose to use it for good."

"It will not be that easy, my friend. Even if you use it for good, the lamp will seek to possess you. You will find that it will consume your time and your energies. Unless you are careful, it will draw you away from the service of your King and you will find yourself living for those things which have no real value. I urge caution, my friend, for the lamp will seek to consume you."

"If the lamp was created by an evil one," one of the workers asked, "how could it possibly be used for good?"

The old man paused. "Let me see if I can explain this so that you will understand it," he said slowly. He thought for a moment. "The gold from which the lamp was fashioned was created by His Majesty, King Emmanuel. The gold itself is not evil, but the lamp was fashioned in such a way as to draw men away from Emmanuel's purposes for them. The evil one of whom I spoke placed the lamps in such locations as to entice men to fall in love with the results that they bring."

"You speak in riddles, old man," one worker growled.

"For that I am sorry, for that was not my intent," the old man replied quietly. He turned again to Demas. "My friend, do not let the lamp possess you." With these words he turned and walked across the crest of the hill, disappearing into the dark shadows of the forest.

"Well, Demas, you heard what he said," one worker joked. "Cast the lamp away before it destroys you."

"If he does, Richard, you'll get it," another replied.

Richard grinned. "Exactly."

Demas stood staring at the golden lamp. At last, he spoke. "If you have the power that I have been told that you have," he said quietly, as if talking to the lamp, "I shall soon have my horse."

The foreman touched him on the shoulder. "Take the lamp to your house for safekeeping," he said, "and then come back and resume work."

Demas nodded and walked away as if in a daze.

The news of Demas' incredible find spread quickly through the village of Mitspah. The golden lamp became the topic of discussion throughout the day. When the quarry crew stopped work and filed into the town square for the noon meal, the townspeople stopped what they were doing and stared at Demas in awe. As Demas found his wife and daughters and sat down with them, he realized that he was surrounded by curious villagers.

"What will you do with the lamp, Demas?"

"Show it to us."

"Will you sell it?"

"Now you can buy that horse you've always wanted."

Finally, the beleaguered man stood to his feet, raising both hands in front of him. "My friends, I am grateful for your interest in my good fortune," he told them. "At the moment, though, I have no plans as to what I shall do with the lamp. But I shall do my best to keep you informed as to my plans for it. And now, if you do not mind greatly, I should like to eat my dinner in peace."

The villagers laughed, congratulated Demas, and drifted away.

His wife leaned close. "Then the stories are true," she whispered. "You did indeed find a golden lamp."

"Aye, they are true," he replied grandly. "When we are home I will show it to you and the girls and tell you the story."

"What about the old man?" she asked, with a worried look. "Was that part of the story also true?"

"Aye," he said simply, not wishing to talk about it.

"Who was the old man?"

He shrugged. "I do not know, wife. Just an old man who

happened along, I suppose."

"But he said—"

"I know what he said," Demas retorted, cutting her off. "Pay no attention to his words. He was just a madman who did not know what he was saying."

"What will you do with the lamp?" Rebecca asked quietly, leaning close to her father.

"Let's discuss it later," he told her, glancing about at those within earshot. "Right now, I wish to eat my dinner."

Unaware of the day's events, Phillip rode in that evening from a day-long hunt. Rebecca was waiting for him outside the gate. "What do you think of Father's lamp?" she cried excitedly as he reined the mare to a stop.

Phillip frowned and swung down from the saddle. "Your father's lamp? Did he make a lamp?"

She stared at him incredulously. "You haven't heard about the lamp?"

He shook his head. "I have been on the hunt since this morning."

The girl was so excited that she could hardly talk. "Father found a lamp this morning, a lamp of solid gold! It was buried in the mountainside, and the lamp was exposed when there was a rockslide. Wait until you see it, Phillip. It's absolutely the most beautiful thing you have ever laid eyes on!"

"The most beautiful thing I have ever laid eyes on is standing before me," he replied.

She blushed. "Seriously, wait until you see this lamp. It appears to be made of solid gold, and it is magnificent, with intricate images of castles and lilies and unicorns engraved upon it. Phillip, it is the most splendid thing that I have ever seen!"

"Where did it come from?"

"Father dug it from the quarry this morning," she replied, brushing a strand of dark hair from her eyes. "As I said, there was a rockslide, which exposed the lamp. Father saw it and dug it from the side of the mountain."

Phillip frowned. "The lamp was encased in solid rock?"

She nodded. "Apparently."

"That's strange. I wonder where it came from."

A strange light played in her eyes. "Everyone in the village is talking about it, Phillip. Father says that he thinks the lamp is made of solid gold, and if it is, he will use it to buy a horse." She clasped her hands together in delight. "Oh, Phillip, isn't it exciting?"

He smiled. "Your father has his heart set on buying a horse, so I hope that he's not disappointed." A thoughtful look crossed his face. "I wonder where the lamp came from. This is the strangest thing that I have ever heard."

Rebecca sighed. "There's more to the story, and this may be the strangest part. Moments after Father found the lamp, a peculiar old man appeared from nowhere and warned him to get rid of it."

"What do you mean he appeared from nowhere? Who was he?"

She shook her head. "No one knows. Father says that just a moment after he had the lamp in his hands, the old man was shaking his arm and telling him to throw the lamp away."

Phillip frowned. "He couldn't have just appeared out of nowhere. Didn't anyone see him walk into the quarry?"

"The other quarrymen said that they didn't see the old man until he was at Father's side, warning him not to keep the lamp."

"Where is the old man now?"

"He walked into the forest."

"Why did he tell your father not to keep the lamp?"

Rebecca paused. "Well, he said that the lamp would try to control Father. 'Consume' is the word he used, I believe. He said that the lamp has some sort of power; in fact, he told Father that it would bring him prosperity."

Phillip laughed. "That doesn't sound too bad."

"The man told Father that the lamp could be used for good or evil, and that if Father was not careful, the lamp would bring a curse upon him and his family."

"That is the most incredible story that I have ever heard." He studied her face. "Are you sure you're not just making all this up?"

Rebecca shook her head. "It really happened, Phillip. Wait until you see the lamp and you'll know that I'm telling the truth."

"I do not doubt you," he assured her. "Where is the lamp now?"

"Father hid it in the house, but I don't know where. He's afraid that someone might try to steal it."

"Have you seen it?"

She nodded eagerly. "It's magnificent, Phillip, the most beautiful thing I have ever seen!"

He mounted the mare. "I would like to see the lamp," he told her. "Will your father show it to me?"

Moments later Rebecca and Phillip entered the humble, two-room cottage where Rebecca and her family lived. "Phillip would like to see the lamp, if you will show it to him," Rebecca told her father. She gave Phillip a mischievous smile. "He doesn't seem to believe my story about your unusual find."

"I didn't say that!" Phillip protested, and then realized that Rebecca was teasing him.

"Can we trust him?" Demas asked with a straight face. "The lamp is a treasure; I cannot show it to everyone who asks, you know."

"Father!"

Demas smiled suddenly. "Of course we will show it to him." He hurried into the back room and reappeared moments later, carrying a small golden lamp, which he carefully placed on the table.

"Isn't it the most beautiful thing you ever saw?" Mira exclaimed, moving close to Phillip and placing a small arm across his shoulder. "Father says that Fate has smiled upon us."

Phillip sat in awe as he studied Demas' unusual find. In the subdued light of the little cottage, the gold of the magnificent lamp gleamed as if it were made of fire. The lamp was not lit, yet still it seemed that it illuminated the room.

"May I touch it?"

"Certainly," Demas said proudly, grinning as he exhibited his treasure. "You may hold it if you wish."

The golden lamp was warm to the touch as Phillip picked it up. Immediately a stirring sensation swept over him. The lamp seemed a living thing, and he felt himself strangely drawn to it. As he held the lamp, a variety of emotions surged within his soul. At first he felt a thrill of excitement and then a sensation of contentment and well-being. Within moments he found himself desiring to possess the lamp as his own. He actually had to resist the urge to turn and run away with the splendid golden vessel.

"It's magnificent, is it not?' Rebecca's voice broke through his thoughts and he started, guilty at having entertained the idea of bolting with the lamp.

"That it is," he said quietly. Still resisting the urge to steal the valuable object, he forced himself to place it back upon the table, but he found that he could not take his eyes from it. His finger began to trace the outlines of the images engraved in the gold. "The workmanship is marvelous. Lions and castles and unicorns and..." His eye fell upon the symbol of a cross and a crown engraved in the lustrous metal. "Look, this is King Emmanuel's own coat of arms."

Demas picked the lamp up and studied it. "You're right, that it is. I didn't see that before."

"I saw it," Mira declared, but her comment went unnoticed.

"Did the lamp at one time belong to King Emmanuel?" Rebecca asked, looking from Phillip to Demas.

Her father shrugged. "Perhaps it did."

"Where do you think it came from?" Phillip asked.

"I would give anything to find out," Demas replied.

Phillip reached out and gently took the lamp from Demas' grasp. Immediately the sensations swelled within him. "What are you going to do with it?"

"This treasure will buy me a horse," the man replied, rubbing his hands together with glee. Phillip glanced at Demas and saw that a change had taken place. The man's eyes held a haunted, tortured look, and his face glowed with a mysterious, unearthly light. "I will buy ten horses, twenty horses, a hundred horses! I will build a bigger house. I will have olive gardens and vineyards and...and servants! I will be the wealthiest man in the village!"

Like a cold draft from an open window, a chill seemed to sweep across Phillip's soul and a specter of danger danced within his mind. *The lamp does indeed have some sort of power*, he realized. *The old man may have been right.*

Chapter Nine

"You won't believe what happened today," Rebecca told Phillip a few days later as they strolled within the half-finished walls of the Castle of Hope. The workers had finished their tasks and gone home for the evening, and except for two soldiers standing guard, the castle was deserted. "Father received an order for a thousand water vessels! Think of it. A thousand!"

"A thousand vessels," Phillip echoed. "That would amount to quite a bit of money."

"Aye," the girl replied, "and not only that, but the merchant who placed the order insisted on paying in advance. Father has hired workers to help with the order and he bought the horse that he has been wanting for so long."

"I am happy for him," the young man said. "I hope he enjoys it. Did he sell the golden lamp?"

"Well, that's the strange thing," the girl responded. "Father took the lamp to the city intending to sell it. He found a buyer who gave him a good price: one hundred gold coins. Father put the money in his purse and then found a place to buy some food. When he opened the pouch, the money was there, and along with it he found the golden lamp!"

Phillip grimaced. "The lamp had returned? Rebecca, that's impossible!"

"Tell Father that," the girl answered. "He insists that's how it happened."

Phillip shook his head. "There's something mighty strange about that lamp."

"Wait until you hear the rest," the girl responded. "Just as Father discovered that the lamp was once again in his possession, a merchant approached him and asked if he were not a crockery merchant. Phillip, he didn't even know who Father was! How could he have known that he was a crockery merchant?"

"And he's the one who placed the huge order for the water vessels?"

Rebecca nodded. "Aye."

"That is strange." He frowned. "There are some things about that lamp that are beginning to trouble me. It almost seems..." He fell silent.

"Almost seems what?"

He turned to face her. "It almost seems that the old man was right."

Rebecca nodded. "It worries me." She grimaced. "Let's talk about something else."

Phillip surveyed the outer curtain walls of the castle. "They're making good progress," he observed. "The north outer curtain is nearly completed, and the other three walls have been started."

"And the towers are going up quickly, too," Rebecca said, pointing. "Master James says that they will start work on the gatehouses and drawbridge next week. Once the outer curtain wall is completed, the inner curtain wall is next."

"Let's go to the top of the north wall," Phillip suggested. "We'll get the same view that the sentries will when they are guarding the castle."

"How would we get up there? The walls are so tall!"

"We'll simply walk up the ramps on the scaffolding."

Moments later Phillip and Rebecca stood atop the castle wall, silently surveying the panorama before them. "It's a lovely spot for a castle, isn't it?" Rebecca remarked. "I'm glad that Master James chose this location."

"He didn't choose it for the beautiful view," Phillip reminded her. "He chose this location because it can easily be defended against an enemy, and because it affords a good defensive view of the countryside. The Castle of Hope is being built for our protection, remember? If Argamor's knights attack the village again, we'll have a place of safety."

"Master James has told us that King Emmanuel plans for us to build our lives around the castle," Rebecca added. "The Castle of Hope will be a place of safety during an attack, but it will also be a place to meet together to learn of King Emmanuel and to praise his greatness. It will be a place where young boys will be trained to be knights and young girls will be trained to serve. The life of the village will revolve around the activities of the castle."

"The Castle of Hope will become an important part of our lives, I am sure," Phillip replied. He yawned and stretched. "Let's head for home, shall we? I plan to ride quite a distance on the hunt tomorrow, and I want to get to bed early."

"Whoa! Easy there, fellow," Paul called to the lumbering ox as he pulled a heavy cartload of wood down the hill from the forest. "Slow down a bit, fellow, or the load will get away from you." Spotting a horseman approaching, he led the ox to the side of the road to let the man pass.

The rider reined in. "Paul, how are you, old friend?"

Paul was startled. "Demas! I didn't even recognize you!" He gazed up at the powerful gray stallion. "So this is the horse you bought. I heard about it in the village. Demas, he's magnificent."

Demas moved the bridle, causing the big horse to side-step. "I've waited for this horse for years, Paul, and he's everything that I thought he would be."

"And look at those clothes! Demas, you're dressing like a nobleman."

The little man tossed his head diffidently. "Life has been treating me well, friend. My business has expanded to the point that I meet myself coming and going. I had to hire some help just to keep up, and then I have expanded my staff twice since then. I'm so busy that I hardly have time to think." He laughed. "But I can't complain, for the money is coming in almost faster than I can count it."

Paul smiled. "I'm glad you're doing well, Demas. I still remember the days when you could scarcely feed your family."

A look of displeasure crossed the merchant's face at this remark, but Paul didn't notice.

"I know you're no longer working in the quarry, and I would imagine that you're thankful for that. What work assignment do you have now?"

"I no longer have time to work on the castle like a common laborer, Paul."

Paul was stunned. "No longer have time to work on the castle?" he echoed. "The Castle of Hope is the King's business, Demas. By building the castle we serve His Majesty. How can you possible be too busy to serve Emmanuel?"

Demas drew himself to his full height. "You're looking at the most successful merchant in all of Mitspah, my friend. I stay busy from morning to night. Like everyone else I think that the castle is a good idea and I'm certainly not opposed to its building, but I simply don't have the time to cut timber or mix mortar or carry stone. I have more important things to do!"

His friend frowned. "Do you really see your business as more important than the Castle of Hope? What business could be more important than the King's business?"

"What I am doing benefits the village," Demas snapped. "I have hired villagers and I pay them good wages. As the business expands I plan to hire even more. It's not as if I have abandoned my friends and neighbors. It's just that I am too busy to engage myself in the actual labor of building the castle."

"His Majesty did not ask for every hour of every day," Paul said quietly. "He merely asked that we provide the labor to build the castle, a few hours each day. And remember, the castle is for our own protection. No one should appreciate that more than you. When the dark knights attacked our village, was it not your daughter that was nearly taken captive?"

"Don't throw that in my face," Demas growled. "I'd rather not dwell on it."

Paul shrugged. "I'm sorry."

"I had better be going." Demas lifted the reins. "I'm a busy man and I have much to do today."

Paul held up one hand. "Tell me about your business before you go."

"Orders for crockery are coming in from everywhere," Demas said proudly, forgetting about the urgency of his busy schedule. "I have hired a number of craftsmen to keep up with production, while I have merchants traveling from city to city to introduce my wares. We can hardly keep up with the sales." He laughed. "It seems that lately everything I touch turns to gold."

"I'm glad that you're doing well," Paul told him again. "Just don't get too busy or too wealthy to have time for an old friend, will you?"

A pained expression crossed the other man's face. "Paul, you know me better than that. How could I forget an old friend like you? We'll always be friends."

"I just wanted to be sure," Paul replied with a laugh.

Demas turned his horse and pointed. "Have you heard about my new house? It's to be built right there among those oaks on the ridge."

Paul stared at him. "On top of the hill? Why there?"

"My home will be the grandest one in the village," the merchant said proudly, "and therefore it ought to be the highest. When my house is finished, anyone approaching the village from the north or the west will see it before they see the village. Or the castle, for that matter. And what a view I will have from up there."

"I'm sure the view will be spectacular," Paul replied, "but what about safety?"

"Safety?"

"How far will your home be from the castle? Five furlongs? Six, perhaps?"

"Aye, and what difference does that make?"

"What if the village is attacked again? Shouldn't your home and family be closer to the castle? Why not build a new home in the village itself? As you know, Master James plans to build the village wall twenty feet high and six feet thick. By building your home in the village, you would have the protection of the wall and you would be close to the castle in the event of an attack."

"The attack was an isolated incident," Demas replied. "Perhaps the dark knights will never return."

Paul stared at him. "We dare not think that way!" he protested. "Argamor is our sworn enemy. He'll do anything in his power to destroy us, our homes, and our families! We do not know when his next attack will come, but we must be prepared. That's why the Castle of Hope is so crucial."

"Well, as I said, I'm not against building it, but I really don't think it is that important." Demas surveyed the ridge where he intended to build his house. "My new house will be many times as large as my present one, built of the finest stone. It will be a masterpiece of architecture, a work of art immortalized in stone. The very sight of it will enhance the village."

"Demas, how will you afford to build a home such as you describe? We are simple peasants, yet you have plans to build a home suitable for a nobleman."

"Speak for yourself," the merchant said indignantly. "I am no peasant—I am the most successful merchant in Mitspah! As I said, lately it seems that everything I touch turns to gold."

"How do you explain that?" Paul asked quietly.

"The golden lamp," Demas replied grandly. "The legend said that the golden lamp would bring prosperity to its owner, and I am finding that to be true. The golden coins are pouring into my hands almost faster than I can spend them, and I believe that it is the power of the lamp!"

Paul was thoughtful. "You think that the lamp brought you this sudden prosperity?"

Demas leaned down from the saddle, gripping the sleeve of Paul's tunic. "Come with me on this journey, Paul. We have been friends since childhood. I will make you the overseer of my affairs. You can build a house beside mine and together we will enjoy the best that life has to offer!" Releasing Paul's sleeve, he straightened in the saddle. "What do you say—will you join me?"

"The legend also said that the power of the lamp would bring a curse," Paul said quietly. "Have you forgotten that?"

"Only if the power were used for evil," Demas retorted. "I'm not planning to use it in that manner." He fingered the reins. "Will you join me, Paul? The golden lamp is bringing me wealth and prosperity, and I am willing to share it with you. We have always been close friends; we have always done so many things together. Come work for me as my overseer, and together we will see where the golden lamp will take us!"

"I cannot let the lamp take me away from the Castle of Hope," Paul replied, "for it seems that is where it is taking you."

"Continue working on the castle if you wish," the merchant told him. "I do not wish to take you away from that. But won't you come with me and become my overseer? I can use you in my business and we can build magnificent homes side by side on the ridge for the entire village to envy. The power of the lamp can prosper both of us."

"My home will be in the shadow of the castle," Paul replied. "I do not think it wise to build on the ridge, so far from the safety of the castle."

"Then build where you will," his friend urged. "We can still work together. Will you join me?"

Paul sighed. "My heart would pull me in that direction, for your friendship means much to me, but for some unknown reason I find myself saying 'no.' Perhaps I am fearful of the legend of the lamp's curse; I do not know. I only know that I cannot join you."

Demas was silent for a long moment. "Then I wish you the best. Will you do the same for me?"

"Of course, my friend. I value your friendship, and always will. But be careful—do not allow the golden lamp to consume you, as the old man warned. Beware of the curse."

Two days later, Phillip trudged wearily uphill through a tangle of vines and brambles toward a small, secluded lake that he had discovered a fortnight earlier. On the previous visit he had found numerous tracks of hart and roebuck along the shores of the lake and he could tell that the animals were frequenting the lake for water. The lake was an ideal spot for hunting, but the approach was too overgrown for the mare, so he left her at the bottom of the hill.

Reaching the lake, the young huntsman paused in the shadows of the forest and silently scanned the area. His heart leaped. Far across the lake and well out of bow range, a large hart stood at the edge of the forest. As Phillip watched, the animal advanced cautiously to the water's edge and began to drink, lifting its head every few seconds to scent the air and check for danger. He sighed. The hart would be gone long before he could hike to the other side of the lake.

The young huntsman turned, and then halted, doing his best to stand absolutely still. Forty yards away, another hart was cautiously making its way to the water. The animal was well within bow range, but there was an abundance of brush and small trees between the young archer and his quarry. On any shot he made from this vantage he would take a chance on having his arrow deflected by a branch or twig. He decided to move closer.

Stay where you are, he silently willed the hart. *The village of Mitspah can use you for dinner.*

The hart reached the water's edge, scanned the area, and then lowered its head to drink. Phillip used that moment as an opportunity to fade into the brush, intending to approach the animal from behind.

Sensing movement beside him, he slowly turned his head. His heart leaped. Ten yards away, a huge hart stood motionless in the shadows, silently watching him. The animal was enormous, with an impressive spread of antlers. Phillip caught his breath; it looked like the golden hart, the one that he had shot during the earlier hunt!

He held his breath, not daring to move as he studied the magnificent creature with the gold-colored fur. The hart had a vivid scar on its flank; it had been wounded previously. There was no longer any doubt in his mind—the huge deer was the same one from which he had removed his arrow after shooting it. It had somehow come back to life before he could retrieve its carcass. *So it wasn't dragged away by the cougar after all,* he told himself.

The golden hart watched him for what seemed like an eternity. Phillip didn't move. Finally, the hart turned its head away from him and he used the opportunity to quietly slide an arrow from his quiver. Slipping the arrow onto the bowstring, he silently pulled back to full draw. At that moment, the hart turned back to face him.

He released his arrow and then stared in astonishment. The arrow sped true to its mark to strike—empty air. Without moving, the golden hart had simply vanished an instant before the arrow reached it.

His heart pounded as he ran forward. Sure enough, the animal's tracks were plainly evident, so the golden hart was more than just a phantom or an image of his imagination. But how could it have vanished before the arrow struck it? He spent the next ten minutes searching for the arrow, but failed to find it.

Phillip sighed. Perhaps it was best to return to his horse and hunt elsewhere. He headed downhill. Thirty yards from the mare, he killed a large buck.

An hour later as he reached the village, he noticed an unusual amount of activity at the quarry. He could hear the shouts of numerous people down in the quarry itself and saw scores of villagers rushing up the hillside toward it. Turning the mare, he rode toward the site.

"What has happened?" he called to a farmer dashing up the slope. "What is all the excitement?"

"It's another golden lamp!" the man shouted. "Barnabas found another golden lamp at the quarry!"

Chapter Ten

The minstrel sat in the shade of a huge oak, his fingers absently picking out a cheerful melody on the strings of his lyre as he studied the village in the valley. He noted that the village was quiet and nearly deserted. An occasional figure could be seen strolling the streets, and two or three craftsmen and merchants diligently conducted business, but for the most part the town was empty. He looked skyward; the sun was directly overhead. He frowned in bewilderment. Noon was usually a time of business and activity in a village such as this.

He turned his attention to the farms and fields surrounding the village. Although it was harvest time and the fields and orchards were ready to deliver their bounty, he could see no one working the harvest. He frowned again. "Unless someone gets busy soon, the harvest will be lost," he said aloud, though none was near enough to hear him.

His eye fell upon a half-finished castle in the distance. From his vantage he could see that the north wall was nearly completed, but the towers and gatehouses and battlements were not. The east wall was just a few feet high, and in some places, barely two courses of stone high. Through the empty space where the main gate should stand he could see that the south wall was in similar condition. Knowing that a castle under construction was usually a worksite for hundreds of workers, he was puzzled to see only two stone masons at work on the walls. Two or three other workers were carrying stone or mortar, and there were several smaller figures that he could tell were children, but for the most part, the castle was deserted.

With a crew of eight or ten workers, he thought soberly, *it will take two hundred years to finish this castle! These people must not be taking this project seriously.*

His attention was arrested by a commotion on the hillside to the east. Scores of workers were busily hauling material out of a pit and dumping it down the side of the hill. At this distance it appeared to the minstrel that they were dumping crushed stone. A cacophony of sounds from within the pit told him that scores, perhaps hundreds, of workers were busy there, though it sounded as if there was as much fighting taking place as working.

His fingers ceased their strumming and the lyre fell silent. He shook his head, trying to make sense of it all. Why was the castle nearly abandoned while obviously there was much to be done? Why was the harvest being left to perish in the fields? Why were the streets of the village nearly deserted, while the huge excavation on the hillside swarmed with activity? "It doesn't make sense," he said aloud.

The minstrel spotted a tall, broad-shouldered man making his way up the hill toward him. The stranger was walking slowly, head down, obviously upset about something. As he approached, the man let out a long, mournful sigh and dropped to a seat on a fallen log less than ten paces from where the minstrel sat.

"Good day, my lord," the minstrel called in greeting.

The man was startled. "I—I didn't see you there," he

stammered, visibly shaken by the minstrel's greeting. "I thought I was alone."

"I'm sorry to have startled you," the minstrel replied, "for that was not my intent. Aye, it is a pleasant day, is it not? What a day to serve Emmanuel!"

"Aye, I suppose it is," the tall man agreed reluctantly. "I suppose I hadn't noticed."

"Hadn't noticed?" the minstrel echoed. "Any day is a good day to serve Emmanuel and rejoice in his goodness, but on a crisp autumn day like today, life is pure pleasure!"

The man shrugged. His head was down and he stared at the grass.

"You are downcast, my friend," the minstrel observed, "though I know not yet the cause. My name is Encouragement, and I delight to be in the service of His Majesty, King Emmanuel. How may I be of help to you, my friend?"

"I don't know that you can help, stranger. I too am trying to serve Emmanuel, though it seems that I have failed miserably."

"Failed? How does one fail in the service of the King?"

"I have failed," the man repeated.

"Perhaps you have simply not had the opportunity to finish," the minstrel suggested.

The man shook his head, still staring miserably at the grass. "I have failed, sir, plain and simple. I was given a task by my lord, King Emmanuel, and I have failed him."

"As I said, my lord, my name is Encouragement, and I am here to help. You are downcast and defeated, and perhaps I can be of assistance. His Majesty gave us the gift of music to brighten our days and lift our spirits. Would you mind if I play a song for you?"

The man didn't even look up. "As you wish."

The minstrel's fingers flew as he played a lilting, cheerful melody. Throwing back his head, he lifted his voice in song. The golden tones floated in the air like the voice of a meadowlark. The words of the song gave praise to King Emmanuel.

A tear crept down the cheek of the tall man, but he said nothing.

The minstrel played one song after another, sometimes singing, sometimes simply strumming melodies that spoke to the heart of his discouraged companion. He was ministering to the soul of the stranger, and he knew it. Finally, as the notes of one song died away, the stranger raised his head.

"Thank you, my friend. That was beautiful."

The minstrel smiled. "Music is a gift from our King."

The man nodded. "I know, and it has helped. You and your music have ministered to me, and I thank you."

The musician bowed his head. "I am grateful that I could be of service."

Both men sat silently for several long moments.

At last, the minstrel began to play softly. "Would you care to talk, my friend? I am a good listener, and I am here because I care."

The tall man studied him for a long moment. "You really do care, don't you?"

The minstrel nodded. "I am here to help."

"I am James of Arwyn," the stranger said, speaking slowly and hesitantly. "I am a master engineer. The castle that you see in the distance is called the Castle of Hope. I am building it for my King, Emmanuel."

He fell silent, and Encouragement waited patiently.

"It's a long story, sir. Do you have the time for the telling of it?"

Encouragement smiled. "I have the time."

"The village that you see below us is called Mitspah, meaning 'watchful' or 'watch tower,' though it used to be called Hazah, or 'sleeping.' The village was attacked one evening by a band of Argamor's dark knights and two people were killed. The villagers petitioned Emmanuel to build them a castle. His Majesty commissioned me to design and build it."

"Work on the castle has nearly stopped," Encouragement observed. "What happened?"

"The work started well enough," James replied. "At first, the people of the village were thrilled at the idea of having a castle of their own. King Emmanuel requested that the people work each morning, but many of them responded by working all day. The people had a heart to work, and the castle walls were progressing nicely.

"There were some small setbacks, of course, as there always are when one undertakes a project for His Majesty."

"Setbacks?"

"A saboteur has attacked the castle on several occasions, though the attacks were not severe and the results were of no real consequence. It was as though the attacker or attackers, whoever they were—for we never have found out who did it—were bent on simply discouraging us, rather than completely destroying our work."

"You said 'attacks.' Were there more than one?"

"Aye," James replied. "One time several courses of stone in the curtain wall were knocked down. Not the entire wall, mind you, but just a few courses for a distance of ten yards or so. On another occasion the scaffolding was sabotaged so that it collapsed and my workers fell. Wheels have been pulled off the oxcarts, tools have been damaged, that sort of thing. Never anything major, always just little things here and there. Just enough to keep us looking over our shoulders—if you know what I mean."

Encouragement nodded. "How did your workers respond to the sabotage?"

"It made them angry, of course, for even though we are building for King Emmanuel, they saw this castle as belonging to them. But the attacks didn't seem to discourage them in the least. Morale has always been high among the workers, with a few exceptions, of course."

"So the work was going well."

James sighed. "Aye. And then Demas found the lamp."

"The lamp?"

"A golden lamp," James explained. "Demas was a crockery merchant, but his sales were few and he struggled just to feed his family. When the work was started on the Castle of Hope, Demas was assigned to work as a quarryman, though he hated the work and complained frequently to anyone who would listen. He was working in the quarry one day and dug a golden lamp from the side of the mountain. The workers tell me that the lamp was encased in solid rock, yet Demas apparently was able to dig it free without damaging it."

"How did the lamp affect the building of the castle?"

James sighed again. "Legend says that the lamp would bring prosperity to its owner. Apparently, that is what happened. Within a few days of finding the lamp, Demas began to prosper, and today is a very wealthy man."

He turned and pointed. "Do you see the elaborate stone houses on the crest of the hill? The largest one is the one belonging to Demas. It is almost finished and he and his family will soon move in.

"A few weeks later, another lamp was found in the quarry by a farmer. As you might guess, today he is also a wealthy man. Anyone who finds a lamp begins to prosper almost immediately."

"So more than two have been found?" Encouragement asked.

"Thirteen so far. And without exception, every finder is now well on the way to great prosperity."

"And now the rest of the villagers are determined to find lamps of their own," the minstrel guessed. "That's why the quarry now swarms with activity, though the town and castle seem nearly deserted."

James nodded. "With a few exceptions, the villagers now have their eyes on wealth and prosperity."

"They have abandoned the service of their King for the hopes of financial gain."

"Exactly."

"And work on the Castle of Hope has come to a standstill."

"Nearly."

The minstrel was silent for a moment or two as he pondered James' story. At last, he spoke. "Would you tell me why you are so downcast? You look and act like a man who has lost all hope."

"Sir, I have just told you," James responded with a trace of irritation in his voice. "I was commissioned by His Majesty to build the Castle of Hope, but the workers have lost heart and I have failed. That is why I am discouraged."

Encouragement shook his head. "You have not failed, my lord."

"How can you say that?" the builder retorted. "The castle is not finished, is it? Most of my crew have abandoned me, and at the rate we're going, the castle will never be completed! Aye, sir, I have failed!"

"Did not King Emmanuel commission you to plan the castle, organize the laborers, and begin the building?"

"Aye, that he did."

"And what have you done, my lord?"

"I planned the castle, organized the laborers, and began—"

The minstrel interrupted him. "You, sire, have done exactly what your King commanded. I see no failure on your part."

"But the work has come to a standstill, or nearly so, and the castle is not finished. How can you say that I am anything but a failure?"

"The work is His Majesty's, not yours," the minstrel gently reminded the builder. "You have been faithful to carry out your King's orders, and that is all that he requires, sire. There is no failure on your part."

"But the people have lost heart in the project," James protested. "They no longer have a will to work. They are distracted by these...these wretched golden lamps!"

"So they have lost sight of what really matters. They have placed personal gain above service to their King, though the gain they seek is worthless in the next life. They have forgotten that service to their King brings rewards that will follow them all the way to the Golden City of the Redeemed. They have valued the temporal above the eternal, is that not right?"

"Aye, they have," James agreed. "And I have failed to—"

"Their failure is not yours!" Encouragement shouted, leaping to his feet in his excitement. "You have been faithful to the commission given you by His Majesty! You are not a failure!"

James was silent as he thought it through. "Thank you, sir," he said at last. "You have helped me greatly."

The minstrel smiled. "I came to help," he said simply.

James was thoughtful again and fell silent for several minutes. "So what shall I do now?" he asked at length.

"Are you ready to quit?"

"Quit building?" James acted as though the idea offended him. "Nay, sir, I shall never quit! The Castle of Hope was commissioned by His Majesty, and I shall continue building until it is finished. I shall continue, sir, even if I should have to build it by myself!"

Encouragement nodded. "I rejoice to hear you say that, my lord."

James gave a wry smile. "Though I should hope to have some help from the villagers again. After all, it is their castle."

"The Castle of Hope is King Emmanuel's castle," the minstrel reminded him.

"Aye, but you know what I mean."

"Would you like to have help?"

"Help? From what source, sir?"

"I know a young prince with as much zeal in his heart and as much fire in his soul as you, sire," Encouragement replied. "He lives and breathes to serve Emmanuel. Perhaps he can be an inspiration to the villagers and an encouragement to you. Together, you can see the Castle of Hope through to completion."

A huge smile creased the builder's tired face. "Will he come?"

"He will if King Emmanuel sends him," the minstrel replied. "I'll send a petition to His Majesty right now."

Chapter Eleven

The morning sun reflected from glittering swords as eight young squires practiced their swordsmanship on one another. The east bailey of the Castle of Faith echoed with the sounds of the conflict. "For King Emmanuel!" the would-be knights called as they charged each other, wielding their swords with all their might as if they intended to take off each other's heads.

"Take a break, lads," called their mentor, a young prince in the colors of King Emmanuel, as he descended the steps from the battlements of the inner curtain. "Sit down and catch your breath."

Obediently the boys lowered their swords, held the glittering weapons against their sides as they transformed into books, and then placed them carefully inside their doublets, close to their hearts. The prince did the same with his own sword and then took a seat beside the castle well. Sides heaving as they attempted to catch their breath, the boys found seats in the grass around him.

"Prince Josiah," one squire said, "tell us the story of the time you fought the mighty dragon. What was his name? Awtamees?"

Prince Josiah laughed. "Authades," he corrected. "It's a name from the ancient languages, and it means 'self-pleasing' or 'self-willed.' Authades was the most dangerous adversary that I have ever faced. He nearly conquered me."

"Tell us what happened," the squires begged.

"You've heard the story before," Josiah told them.

"Aye, but perhaps we can learn from the retelling," one squire replied. "We are here to learn from you, sire, as we desire to be knights for His Majesty. If you please, sire, tell the tale again."

Josiah shrugged. "All right. Let's see, where should I begin?"

"You were searching for the Crown of Kuros," one boy prompted.

The young prince laughed again. "See? You know the story as well as I do." He paused.

"Please, sire, tell it," the boys begged.

"The Crown of Kuros was cut from a single, flawless diamond," Josiah began. "Possession of the crown determined who would reign within the heart of one person. The enchantress Morphina took the crown from the castle keep because I had failed to obey. After realizing that the loss of the crown was my fault, I was attempting to return the crown to the possession of King Emmanuel."

"And you had to fight the dragon to get the crown back."

"Who's telling the story?" Josiah demanded, and then laughed as the boy ducked his head meekly.

"The dragon Authades," Josiah continued, "was a powerful, fire-breathing monster more than sixty feet long, and he lived in a cavern filled with the bones of dead knights. His scales were like armor; they could turn the sharpest arrows and blunt the strongest spears. His teeth were like swords. Never before había I faced such a formidable adversary."

The squires leaned forward eagerly, eyes fastened on the young prince.

"I entered the dragon's lair with Sir Wisdom at my side, for he had offered to accompany me, and I was glad for his companionship. Shortly after entering the gloom of the cavern I could hear Authades coming for me, and I could smell him, for he has the stench of death about him, but I could not see him. He can render himself invisible for short periods of time.

"The dragon roared with rage, and the sound was so terrifying that I dropped my sword in fear. Sir Wisdom helped me retrieve my sword. When I came face to face with the dragon, he tried to strike fear into my heart by telling me that he had defeated every king and every knight that had dared to stand before him, and he threatened to destroy me. The dragon charged toward me belching blasts of fire. I turned to run, but Sir Wisdom encouraged me to stand firm."

The young prince paused as the images of the fierce battle played within his memory. "During the battle, Authades' head struck me and I again dropped my sword. I retrieved it. I managed to strike a telling blow against the dragon, seriously wounding him. Authades then offered me the crown if I would leave the cavern without killing him, but I refused.

"Suddenly I found myself battling a huge serpent, the Serpent of Selfishness, for in reality, the dragon was the serpent. When I inflicted several wounds to the serpent, he once again became the dragon, attacking me in fury. Praise be to His Majesty, his sword inflicted a terrible wound to the head of the dragon, killing him. The dragon's body melted and I recovered the Crown of Kuros for King Emmanuel. It is safe once again within the keep of the Castle of Faith."

"That was some battle!" one squire declared, his eyes wide

with awe. "Weren't you afraid?"

"In truth, I was terrified," Josiah replied, "but I knew that I had to battle Authades to recover the crown for my King." He turned to the squire who had begged for the story. "And what did you learn, my good squire, from the retelling of the story?"

"You said that the dragon Authades changed himself into the Serpent of Selfishness," the squire responded, "for they were one and the same. So when you were battling the dragon, in reality you were battling your own selfishness?"

"Exactly," Prince Josiah told him. "Our own selfishness is one of the most dreadful foes we face. Selfishness has destroyed many a knight of Emmanuel's, rendering him ineffective in His Majesty's service."

"Josiah." The prince and the young squires turned at the sound of a pleasant voice to see a young woman hurrying across the courtyard. Slender and graceful, Princess Gilda wore her long golden tresses in braids. A long, flowing gown of pale green satin and a shawl of exquisite white lace fluttered about her figure. As usual, her cheerful face was graced by a friendly smile of greeting.

"Gilda! Good morning to you, my fair lady," Josiah greeted her warmly.

"And good morning to you, my handsome prince," Gilda responded. The squires all laughed. Gilda turned to the boys. "And good morning to you, fine squires of the castle. How goes the training this morning?"

"Prince Josiah makes us work too hard," one squire complained. "He makes us battle and battle until we are so tired we can hardly stand up."

"There is no pause to rest in a real battle," Josiah replied, speaking to all the squires. "I want you to be ready when you stand before a real enemy."

"Princess Gilda, are you and Prince Josiah going to get married?" another squire asked abruptly.

Gilda blushed, and then threw a playful glance in Josiah's direction. "The prince hasn't asked me yet."

Josiah laughed and made a sweeping motion with his arm. "Future knights, why don't you take a run to the village and back? That will give me a moment or two to talk with the princess."

Obediently, the squires stood and ran across the courtyard, disappearing through the entrance to the west bailey. Gilda moved closer to Josiah. "How did the practice go today?"

"It went well. I'm working with some fine young boys. Their swordsmanship is something to see."

"Your squires think the world of you. They talk about you constantly. 'Prince Josiah says this; Prince Josiah says that.' They really admire you."

"They have good hearts and they take their training seriously. They'll make good knights for His Majesty." Josiah paused, deep in thought. "You know, seven years ago when I came to the Castle of Faith, I was just about their age. I'll never forget that day. I was a skinny little wretch, nearly starving to death, and perishing under the hand of Argamor. King Emmanuel broke my chains and set me free, adopted me, and brought me here to the castle. I am forever grateful to His Majesty."

Josiah looked at Gilda. "And then I met you."

"Well, sire, is that good or bad?"

"You're the sunshine in my day, my dear Gilda."

Gilda hesitated and then asked, "My prince, what is the answer to the young squire's question?"

"And what question is that?"

"Are we going to get married?"

Josiah turned to face her, looking deeply into her vivid blue eyes. "I've already petitioned the King for permission to marry you. I await his answer."

She studied his face, fearful that he was jesting. "Indeed? Did you really?"

He nodded. "Gilda, there is nothing that I would like better than to spend the rest of my life with you."

"We could serve Emmanuel together."

He nodded again. "I want nothing more."

Gilda sighed and took a step away from Josiah. "Perhaps we can talk of this later. Right now, Sir Faithful would like to see you. He's in the great hall."

"Do you know what he wants?"

"He didn't say. I do know, however, that just this morning he received a messenger from the Golden City. Perhaps King Emmanuel sent a message for you."

Josiah was thoughtful. "When the squires come back, dismiss them for the day, will you? I'll go see what Sir Faithful wants." He looked at her tenderly. "This evening after dinner, will you take a walk with me? We shall talk again of our future together."

She smiled. "My heart shall look forward to it, my prince."

"Sire, you sent for me?" Josiah asked as he approached Sir Faithful in the great hall.

"Aye," the castle steward replied. "This morning the Castle of Faith received a messenger from the Golden City of the Redeemed. His Majesty has planned a special quest for you, if you are willing."

"I delight to do His Majesty's will," the young prince responded eagerly. "What am I to do?"

"Sit down," the castle steward replied. He poured a cup of

water and passed it across the table to Josiah.

"The village of Mitspah, formerly known as 'Hazah,' " Sir Faithful began, "is about six hundred furlongs northeast of here, situated on the banks of Distinction River. Earlier this year Hazah was attacked by a band of Argamor's knights. Two villagers were killed in the attack. The village leaders petitioned King Emmanuel to build them a castle and he has agreed. He sent James of Arwyn to plan and build the castle, which is called the Castle of Hope.

"At first, the building of the castle went well. The villagers had a mind to work and they pitched in willingly. The walls were going up at record speed. There were problems, of course, as there always are when one undertakes a great task for Emmanuel."

Sir Faithful then told the prince about the acts of sabotage. "But in spite of the attacks the townspeople refused to be sidetracked; they continued to build as if nothing had happened."

He sighed. "And then the golden lamps appeared."

"Lamps, sire?" Josiah echoed. "Did you say lamps?"

"Lamps," Sir Faithful repeated. "Golden lamps were found in the quarry by several villagers, and those who found them began to prosper immediately. They are building new homes and acquiring great possessions. Most of the other villagers have now abandoned the building of the castle and are seeking lamps of their own."

Prince Josiah was stunned. "They've abandoned King Emmanuel's work for the sake of material prosperity? Why would they do that?"

"Prosperity can be very enticing," the steward replied. "Emmanuel gave us the ability to work and prosper and get wealth, but Argamor tries to use that to draw mankind away from their service to their King. Emmanuel created the gold, but Argamor fashioned the gold into lamps that are so alluring they draw men away from their real purpose in life."

"Is anyone still working on the castle?"

"Very few," the steward replied. "The partially finished castle stands as a mockery to the name of Emmanuel."

Josiah shook his head sadly. "Argamor's purposes were served far better than if he had attacked the castle builders directly. If the Castle of Hope is not being built, that's exactly what he wanted."

Sir Faithful nodded. "James of Arwyn has tried to rally the workers and renew their interest in the Castle of Hope, but to no avail. He has become very discouraged. That's why His Majesty sent for you."

"Me, sire? What can I do?"

"King Emmanuel wants you to go to Mitspah and assist James in the building of the Castle of Hope."

"In what way, sire?"

"You have a zeal to serve Emmanuel, and we want you in some way to impart that zeal to the hearts of the people of Mitspah. Find some way to draw their hearts back to the work of their King. Encourage them to resume the building of the castle. At the same time, we want you to find the saboteur or saboteurs and bring their interference to an end."

Prince Josiah let out his breath in a long, slow sigh. "That's a big assignment, sire. I am but one person, yet I am to motivate an entire village to serve their King once again?"

"Aye, but His Majesty has commissioned you for this quest," Sir Faithful reminded him gently, "so he has also equipped you for the task. Go trusting in him, and you shall be successful. His strength is your strength. You know that, Josiah."

The young prince nodded. "Aye, sire, that I do. When am I to leave on this journey?"

"Immediately."

Prince Josiah took a sip of water. "Will you do something for me, sire?"

"Aye," the old man replied, "name it and it shall be done."

"Will you tell Gilda where I am going? She is expecting to take a walk with me this evening, but I shall not be there." He hesitated. "Sire, I cannot break a promise to her."

"I will tell her. She will understand that the King's business is priority." The steward smiled. "She will be waiting for you when you return."

He placed his hand on Josiah's arm. "There will be opposition, of course, and this quest may be one of great danger. Argamor does not want the Castle of Hope to be built, and he will oppose you. Be sober, be vigilant, for your adversary is as a roaring lion, seeking whom he may devour."

"I shall be watchful, sire, and I shall go trusting in Emmanuel. My heart rejoices to serve my King in this way."

Unnoticed by Prince Josiah or Sir Faithful, a figure dressed as a female servant had been quietly sweeping the floor of the great hall. Head down as though absorbed in her work, she had been silently listening to every word. As the young prince followed the castle steward from the great hall, the woman slipped unseen through a side door and hurried toward the castle entrance.

Chapter Twelve

Young Mira's heart pounded with excitement as she rode a gentle black-and-white pony along the road leading to the quarry. Spotting a group of children in the roadway ahead, she reined to a halt beside them.

"Mira," one girl called, "whose pony is that?"

"He's mine," Mira replied grandly, though without a trace of arrogance or pride. "Father bought him for me."

"May we ride him?" a dozen voices chorused.

The friendly girl immediately swung down from the saddle. "Aye, you may," she replied generously, for she was a kind-hearted soul and did not know what it was to be selfish. "I will lead him, though, for he does not yet know you."

"May I go first?" Diana, the baker's daughter, asked politely.

"Aye," Mira replied, and helped her mount the little pony. Mira took the reins and led the patient animal carefully along the road. The crowd of village children chattered excitedly as they followed along behind.

"I wish my father could find a golden lamp," one girl said wistfully, "and then perhaps I could have a pony as grand as this."

"My father would buy me a full-size horse," a boy declared

officiously. "He told me so! He says that if he finds a golden lamp he'll buy Mama a new house and buy me a horse."

"My father will be the next to find a lamp," another boasted. "Wait and see."

"There's no way to know that," a tall boy scoffed. "Fate decides who gets the lamps. My father said so."

"My father says that the lamps are found by those who work the hardest for them," another replied.

"May I have a turn now?" a thin-faced girl asked a moment later. "Diana has ridden more than a furlong."

Mira brought the pony to stop while Diana dismounted and the new rider took her place. "Thank you, Mira," Diana said sweetly. "Oh, I do hope that Papa finds a golden lamp so that we can buy a pony like this one!"

The children took turns riding the gentle little pony, which to most of them was as grand as the most magnificent war-horse. Mira was thrilled to realize that she now possessed something that could make her friends happy, and she delighted in allowing them to ride her new possession. In her innocence, she failed to see the looks of jealousy that appeared on some of the young faces.

Phillip paused at the entrance to a steep, rocky canyon. He rested the end of his longbow in the sand as he studied the ground for tracks. He had been tracking the hart for more than an hour now, and he was tired, hungry and thirsty. His heart leaped. His quarry had entered the canyon—the abundance of fresh tracks told him that—and he knew from previous hunts that the canyon ended in a sheer precipice that no animal could climb. The hart was cornered and would soon be his.

Fitting an arrow to the bowstring, the young huntsman pulled back to quarter draw and then started cautiously forward. Step by step he crept into the canyon, carefully studying every tree and bush, every rock and windfall and shadow as he searched for the hart. His own heart pounded. The animal could not escape; today would be the day.

A twig snapped to his left and he whirled, pulling to full draw as he did. But there was nothing there. Puzzled, he relaxed the tension on the bowstring and resumed his walk into the canyon. The crisp, fresh tracks at his feet told him again that the hart had indeed just passed that way.

His mind reviewed the hunts of the last few days. Somehow he had managed to spot the enormous golden hart nearly every day of the previous week, but he had never been able to get close enough for a shot. In some mysterious way the big deer had eluded him each and every time. He shook his head. It didn't make sense. His skills as a hunter should have brought him within bow range on almost every occasion, but so far, it just hadn't happened.

His heart raced. Today would be different. The golden hart had trapped himself by fleeing into a canyon that had no other exit.

The young huntsman crept silently forward. The afternoon breeze stirred in the treetops; the leaves whispered to each other like old friends sharing secrets. A young rabbit bounded across the trail, paused and regarded Phillip with curious eyes, and then bounded away into the brush before the hunter could raise his bow.

Consider yourself fortunate, Phillip silently told the rabbit, *for I am in pursuit of bigger game. Were I not on the track of a trophy hart, you would be in my game bag right now!*

He thought about the fact that he had not made a single

kill that week. The elusive hart had distracted him from his purpose in the hunt: to provide food for the village and for the work crew building the castle. *I'll take the hart today,* he told himself, *and then I'll go back to hunting for the sole purpose of putting meat on the tables of Mitspah.*

What will Rebecca think when she sees the giant hart draped across the back of my saddle? What will Demas and the other villagers think? They seem so eager to hear the stories of my hunts—wait till they see this magnificent trophy! Phillip grinned in anticipation.

Just then he heard a loud crashing in the brush ahead and his heart raced. The hart! Pulling the arrow to half draw, he hurried toward the sound. Beads of sweat popped out on his brow and he was amazed to realize that he was trembling with excitement. In another moment or two the magnificent hart would be his. Crouching low, he crept through a canebrake and stepped cautiously over a fallen log. Moving slowly, noise-lessly, he entered the small clearing from which the sound had originated.

Moving only his eyes, he scanned the area in bewilderment. The clearing was empty—there was no hart.

Sensing that he was not alone, Phillip slowly turned his upper body. His heart pounded. His quarry was directly behind him, standing motionless in the middle of the trail less than ten yards away! The golden hart was so close that Phillip could clearly see the scar on his left flank.

The young huntsman held his breath. His mind raced. The hart was watching him—if he moved a muscle, the wary animal would instantly bound away before he could get his bow into position for a shot. *How could I have passed by him without seeing him?* he berated himself. *I had him cornered with no escape, but now somehow he's behind me.*

His heart was in his throat as he turned slowly, slowly, slowly, moving so painstakingly slow that the motion was almost imperceptible. The hart stood motionless, seemingly watching him the entire time. When his shoulders were at right angles to the magnificent animal, the young huntsman slowly pulled his bowstring back to full draw.

Twang! The arrow sped from the bowstring. Phillip's heart leaped as the missile struck the huge deer's flank barely an inch from the scar. His elation instantly turned to astonishment as the arrow continued on to embed itself deeply in a tree trunk directly behind the animal. Still standing, the golden hart slowly faded from view as if it had been merely an apparition. The arrow had passed through without wounding the magnificent creature.

Puzzled, Phillip strode forward with longbow in hand to investigate. His heart pounded as he studied the ground where just moments before the animal had stood. The hart's tracks were visible in the soft soil, clear and easily distinguishable. He shook his head in bewilderment. The massive deer was not merely a figment of his imagination.

Letting out his breath slowly, he turned and made his way back to the walnut grove where the mare waited patiently. Unseen by the young huntsman, the golden hart watched silently from a nearby thicket.

Andrew and Nathaniel hurried down the village street, eager to reach the castle site. "We'll have to hurry or we'll be late," Andrew told his friend. "We should have left the house five minutes ago. Most of the masonry crew is probably already there, and they'll be waiting for us."

Nathaniel nodded. "I'm sorry that breakfast took so long,"

he apologized. "I should have milked the cow for Mama, just to save time."

As they reached the village square, several boys joined them. "Where are you heading in such a hurry?" one asked.

"We're going to work on the castle, of course," Andrew replied. "If we don't hurry, we're going to be late."

"Why are you still working on the castle? We're going to the quarry to search for golden lamps."

"Come with us," another urged. "You might be the one to find a lamp!"

"King Emmanuel wants us to work on the Castle of Hope," Andrew replied, without breaking stride. "His work is more important than searching for a golden lamp."

Nathaniel kept pace with Andrew. "Why don't you fellows come with us and work on the castle instead of searching for a lamp?"

"Not us," one of the boys replied, as the group veered away and headed for the quarry. "We're going to search for lamps. If someone finds a lamp today, it might be one of us!"

"They've lost sight of what's really important," Andrew said sadly as he and Nathaniel watched the other boys head up the hill. "Serving our King is more important than finding a golden lamp."

Nathaniel nodded. "Aye, and when King Emmanuel returns and takes us to the Golden City of the Redeemed, we'll be glad that we stayed true."

Prince Josiah paused in the shade of a scarlet maple. The day was crisp and cool and the hillside was alive with vivid, vibrant color. Fiery red maples, golden tamarack and birch, orange sugar maples, purple ash and butter-yellow hickories all contrasted against the deep blue and green of the spruce and pines. The woods seemed alive. Josiah could not remember having ever seen a prettier day.

Pulling a book from within his doublet, the young prince opened it, and the pages began to glow with a soft white light. Watching the book carefully, he turned it slowly from side to side, noting which the direction the book was facing when it glowed the brightest. Closing the book and stowing it once again within his doublet, he then rode in the direction indicated by the book.

"How am I to motivate an entire village to serve Emmanuel?" he asked aloud. "What am I to say that can change a man's heart and cause him to focus on service to his King rather then seeking wealth and prosperity? My lord, my King, I fear that I am unsuited to this task."

Drawing the book once again from his doublet, he opened it and withdrew a parchment from within. Thoughtfully, he wrote a message to King Emmanuel:

> *"Your Majesty,*
>
> *Help me, my King, to somehow find a way to show the villagers that service to you brings rewards that will last forever. Help me to show them that any wealth and possessions that they may acquire by means of the golden lamps will be taken from them the moment they leave for the Golden City of the Redeemed. Help them to see that prosperity is only temporary, while true riches are to be found by serving you.*
>
> *Your grateful son, Josiah."*

He rolled the parchment tightly and released it, watching in satisfaction as the petition disappeared over the treetops.

Night was falling over the kingdom of Terrestria as the young prince rode into a clearing on the top of a small hill. He glanced heavenward. The evening stars were just beginning to make their appearance and he scanned the heavens, searching for one of the constellations that bore witness to the majestic character of Emmanuel. To the north he spotted his favorite, the constellation depicting Emmanuel as a shepherd.

"Have you lost your way, my lord?" The voice was friendly, but it startled Josiah so that he jumped in fright.

A horseman reined in close to the young prince. "A thousand pardons, my lord, for I did not intend to frighten you. I simply came to see if I might be of assistance. Have you lost your way?"

Josiah shook his head. "I merely paused for a moment's reflection," he replied. "I am on my way to Mitspah."

"Mitspah," the other echoed, and Josiah realized that the rider was a young man about his age. "You are nearly there, my lord, six or eight furlongs at most. But why would you desire to go to Mitspah?"

"I am on business for His Majesty," Josiah explained vaguely, not mentioning the Castle of Hope.

"What business would His Majesty have in Mitspah?" the stranger asked quietly, as if not intending for Josiah to hear. "The village of Mitspah is no more."

"What do you mean, sir?" Josiah asked.

"Perhaps the matter is better explained in the showing than in the telling," the young horseman replied. "Would you follow me to Mitspah?"

"Lead the way," Josiah responded.

"My name is Phillip, and I am from Mitspah," the young man explained, turning his horse toward the southwest. "Until recently, I was the huntsman for the village and for the Castle of Hope." He sighed. "Alas, that is no more."

"I am Josiah, son of His Majesty, King Emmanuel," the young prince replied, turning his own horse to follow Phillip's. "I am sent to assist in the building of the Castle of Hope. What has happened to the village?"

"I would rather show you than tell you. Follow me."

Josiah followed the young huntsman across the crest of the hill and into the darkness of a dense forest. The moon was just beginning to peek over the hills to the east, but its silvery beams could not penetrate the darkness; Josiah caught only an occasional glimpse of its silver face. He stayed close to Phillip, barely able to make out the dark form of his horse.

After a ride of ten minutes the young huntsman reined his horse to the side of the narrow trail. "From this point on the trail is too steep for the horses," he explained, as he dismounted. "We'll have to leave them here." He tied his mount to a tree and Josiah did the same.

The two young men began to climb a rugged, rocky hillside. Scrambling over boulders, climbing over fallen trees, hiking up narrow ravines, they slowly scaled some of the most rugged terrain that Josiah had ever encountered. Within moments, the young prince was huffing and puffing.

"Slow down," he panted. "Let me catch my breath."

"We'll rest for a moment or two," his guide offered. "Being a huntsman, I am accustomed to rugged terrain, but I sometimes forget that not everyone can climb it as easily. I beg your forgiveness."

"I won't hold it against you," Josiah promised with a grin, "but I do appreciate a chance to catch my wind." Hands on his knees, he struggled to catch his breath as he gazed up the side of the mountain. "Is the Castle of Hope being built on top of a mountain? I thought it was situated beside the Distinction River."

"Oh, I'm not taking you to the castle," Phillip replied quickly. "I'm taking you to a point from which we can view it and the village."

"How much farther?"

"We're almost there."

Five minutes later, the two young men walked out on a ledge of rock overlooking a peaceful, moonlit valley. Phillip moved close to Josiah. "The Castle of Hope is to your left," he said, pointing. "See the light-colored outcropping of stone? Once you find that you can make out the outlines of the castle. The village is just to the right of it and slightly closer to us."

The scene below them was breathtaking in its splendor. The valley, bathed in the silver-blue light of the crescent moon, fell away below them in a peaceful panorama of color and contrasting shadows. For a few magical moments, rocks on the hillsides had somehow been transformed into glistening chunks of white silver. The deep purple of the mountains contrasted with the verdant green of the valley floor. In the center, a little stream had become a thin, silver-blue thread winding its way across the lush green carpet of the valley floor. The entire landscape had an ethereal, dreamlike quality.

Josiah gazed across the valley, enthralled by the majestic sight below him. "Where's the castle?" he whispered softly, almost as if he were afraid to speak aloud.

Phillip pointed. "To your left," he replied quietly. "See the stone outcropping?"

Far below, a huge mass of limestone jutted out from the hillside. The blackened remains of a castle contrasted sharply against its stark white face. Josiah stared. The structure was in ruins. Even from this great distance he could see the crumbling walls, the charred gates, the rotting remains of the huge drawbridge. The roof of the great hall had been burned away;

most of the towers and turrets were also roofless. The Castle of Hope was in shambles.

The village had fared no better. The stone wall had been battered down in many places, and the gates were missing altogether. Blackened, roofless shops and cottages stood lifeless and eerie in the moonlight, giving silent testimony to the fact that the village had been destroyed by fire.

A snowy white dove in a nearby elm tree spoke quietly, but Josiah failed to hear him or see him in the darkness.

Viewing the ruins of the castle and the village, the young prince experienced a sinking, nauseous feeling deep within. He had come too late; Emmanuel's castle had been abandoned. "What—what happened?" he asked in a hoarse voice.

"The golden lamps," Phillip replied quietly. "Once the villagers began to find the golden lamps, they lost interest in the Castle of Hope. Now it sits abandoned and lifeless, the home of vile beasts and disgusting birds of prey."

"B-But I was sent by King Emmanuel to assist in the building," Josiah stammered. "I was to remind the villagers that the Castle of Hope is His Majesty's project and to encourage them to begin building anew."

Phillip shrugged. "You might as well return home," he said sadly. "You came too late."

Chapter Thirteen

Josiah stared into the flames of his campfire. Two golden trout sizzled on a spit suspended above the fire; Josiah had caught them on a hand line. The aroma of baking trout filled the little clearing, but the young prince's mind was not on the fish.

He thought about what he had seen from the ledge atop the mountain. The Castle of Hope had been abandoned; its walls and gates and towers lay in charred shambles. His mission for King Emmanuel had not turned out as he had hoped. He sighed. Was this quest to end in failure before it even started?

A twig broke with a loud snap and he jumped, quite startled by the sound. He turned, but all he saw were the reflections of the flames dancing on the trunks of the trees. *I must be tired,* he told himself. *I'm hearing noises that aren't even there.*

He turned back to the fire and then cried out in alarm. Before him stood a dark knight with sword drawn. In an instant the blade of the sword was pressing painfully against Josiah's neck. The young prince stared up into the dark knight's leering face and his stomach tightened. His legs began to shake. The blood began to pound in his head. His chest felt so tight that he could scarcely breathe.

"We'll just take that magnificent shield of yours, young

prince," the knight said, gesturing toward Josiah's Shield of Faith with his free hand. "Those jewels must be worth a king's ransom! Hand the shield over to me or I'll run you through." Three more dark knights appeared behind him as he spoke.

Josiah glanced at the shield with its row of seven lustrous jewels, emblems of his quest to reach seven castles for King Emmanuel. The shield lay just out of reach, propped up against the log on which he sat. His heart sank. He could never surrender the shield, but he would die if he refused.

"Hand it to me," the dark knight demanded again.

Moving slowly and cautiously, the young prince raised his right hand to show that he was not resisting and then leaned across and picked up the shield with his left. As he raised the Shield of Faith, of its own accord it leaped upward and forward, striking the dark knight's sword and hurling him backward. Startled beyond words, Josiah nevertheless had the presence of mind to roll immediately to his feet, drawing his sword as he did.

He found himself facing not one but four drawn swords. "Drop your sword and hand me the shield, foolish prince," the leader of the dark knights snarled. "One more foolish move and I take off your head." All four knights took a menacing step forward.

"I bear the sword of Emmanuel and the Shield of Faith," Josiah countered. "Your defeat is already accomplished."

"Surrender the shield or die!" the enemy knight growled. He raised his sword, intending to take off Josiah's head.

Josiah saw the blow coming and simply raised his Shield of Faith, easily deflecting the attack. With two quick thrusts of Emmanuel's sword he ended the enemy knight's life.

Howling with rage, the three enemy knights were upon him, swinging their swords in fury. The Shield of Faith protected the young prince from their savage assault, deflecting blow after blow. Time after time, Josiah's own sword inflicted wounds upon the adversaries, but not once did their blades touch him. Within minutes, all four dark knights lay dead upon the ground.

"King Emmanuel, the victory is yours!" Josiah cried, dropping to one knee in gratitude. "Your mighty sword and your invincible shield have wrought a victory over the evil ones."

Holding his sword against his side until it transformed into a book, he then opened the cover and withdrew a parchment. With a heart of gratitude he wrote a petition of thanksgiving to his King. Rolling the parchment tightly, he released it and watched it streak through the darkness of the night as it sped to the throne room in the Golden City. He then replaced the book within his doublet.

"I'll return home to the Castle of Faith in the morning," he said aloud with a sigh. "I might as well get a night's sleep here first."

"What's this I hear about returning to the Castle of Faith?" demanded a familiar voice, and the young prince jumped in fright. An elderly man strode into the circle of light cast by the campfire.

"Sir Wisdom!" Josiah exclaimed.

The nobleman dropped to a seat on the log beside Josiah. "So you plan to return to the Castle of Faith tomorrow, do you?"

"Aye, sire." Josiah turned the spit, rotating the trout over the fire. "The Castle of Hope has been destroyed and abandoned, as has the village of Mitspah. I simply came too late, sire."

"Destroyed and abandoned, you say." Sir Wisdom frowned. "And just how did you come by this information?"

"I saw the castle tonight with my own eyes," the young prince replied. "One of the villagers, a young huntsman by the name of Phillip, took me to the site. It was disheartening, sire. The walls were broken down, the gates burned, most of the roofs missing. The village was in the same sad state, sire, and there was not a soul anywhere. I came too late to help."

"You say the Castle of Hope had been burned?"

"Aye, sire. There was nothing left of the gates and drawbridge but charred timbers. The roof of the great hall had been almost completely burned away, as had the roofs of most of the towers and other buildings. The castle and the village had both been destroyed by fire, sire."

"The drawbridge at the Castle of Hope has not yet been built," Sir Wisdom said quietly.

Josiah stared at him. "Aye, sire, but it has. I saw it tonight, though there is almost nothing left of it."

"The Castle of Hope is still in the early stages of construction," the old man told him. "The gatehouses are not built, no towers are finished, and work has not even started on the drawbridge!"

Prince Josiah was embarrassed, but he felt it necessary to correct the old man. "Sire, I saw the castle tonight. The gates and drawbridge were completed, sire, though they had been nearly destroyed by fire. And the towers—"

Sir Wisdom held up both hands. "Josiah, Josiah, listen to me. I know whereof I speak. Work has not even started on the gates and drawbridge of the Castle of Hope."

"But, sire, I saw—"

"What you saw," the old man replied with a hint of a smile, "was not the Castle of Hope. Tonight you were deceived by a very clever adversary."

"Not the Castle of Hope? How do you know, sire?"

"Work has not yet begun on the gates and drawbridge of the Castle of Hope. If you saw such things at the castle tonight, reason tells us that it was not the Castle of Hope that you were viewing."

"Then what castle was it?"

"Perhaps it was the Castle of Confidence, for that castle was destroyed by Argamor's forces many years ago. As I remember, it was burned."

The young prince was puzzled. "Then why did Phillip lie to me? He said it was the Castle of Hope."

"I know Phillip of Mitspah," Sir Wisdom told him. "He would never lie to you."

"But why did he tell me that the burned-out castle was the Castle of Hope, if in truth it was not? Is that not a lie?"

"Aye, but Phillip did not tell you that."

"Aye, sire, but he did! He said—" Josiah stopped in midsentence and stared at his companion. "Are you saying that the man I saw was not Phillip? Then who was it?"

"You have met her before," the nobleman said impishly. "Did you not recognize her?"

"Her?" Josiah was confused, and then suddenly the light dawned. "Morphina? Was it the enchantress, Morphina?"

Sir Wisdom nodded. "Exactly."

Josiah groaned. "She had me fooled completely! She told me that she was Phillip, a young huntsman from Mitspah, and I believed her!"

"Among deceivers, she's the best of the best. She has led astray some of Emmanuel's choicest knights."

Josiah thought it through. "What was her purpose?"

"She serves Argamor, and Argamor does not want the Castle of Hope to be built. You were sent to help build the castle, so she was sent to keep you from your mission."

"How did she intend to do that?"

"Simply by discouraging you. If she could convince you

that the Castle of Hope was beyond hope you would return home and therefore fail to accomplish Emmanuel's purpose in sending you. She almost succeeded, did she not?"

"Almost," the young prince sheepishly admitted. "But for you, sire, she would have!" He was frustrated. "I should have recognized her."

"Now you know who you are up against." Sir Wisdom stood to his feet. "You're still seventy furlongs from the castle. Get some rest and finish your journey in the morning. Good night, Prince Josiah." With these words he was gone.

Josiah rose early the next morning. After catching and roasting two more trout, he was on his way, riding from his campsite just as the sun was peeking above the trees.

An hour later, Josiah reined the mare to a stop while he consulted the book. A horse neighed and he looked up to see a magnificent gray horse approaching. The rider was a small man dressed in gaudy brocade.

"Good day, my lord," the rider addressed him. "Fine autumn day, is it not?"

"Aye, that it is, sire," Josiah answered. "'Tis indeed a fine day to serve His Majesty."

A strange look crossed the little man's face, but he said nothing.

"That's a magnificent horse, sire," Josiah told the stranger, "perhaps one of the finest in all of Terrestria."

The man's face showed his pleasure at the young prince's words. "I thank you, my lord. It has indeed been a pleasure to own an animal as fine as this." He studied Josiah, noting his elegant clothing and the royal coat of arms upon his shield. "Are you traveling through the region, my lord?"

"I'm on business for His Majesty," Josiah replied. "Would you know how far I am from the village of Mitspah?"

"Mitspah? My lord, for thirty-five years I have made my home in Mitspah."

"Indeed. Then you can tell me how far we are from your village."

The little man paused. "It is not far, perhaps five or six furlongs. You are visiting Mitspah at a good time—prosperity has just come to our little village. We are building new homes and buying magnificent horses; our shops and farms and businesses are flourishing and making money faster than ever before. In fact, my own business has exploded; orders for my wares are coming in faster than I can possibly fill them.

"But I cannot complain, my friend, for I am making money almost faster than I can count it." He laughed. "And that is what really matters, is it not?"

The little man eyed Josiah. "I suppose that business brings you to Mitspah—am I correct?"

Josiah nodded. "I am on business for His Majesty, King Emmanuel."

"And what business is that, my lord?"

"King Emmanuel has sent me," Josiah replied, "to assist in the building of the Castle of Hope."

"Aye, the Castle of Hope. Well, my lord, good day to you." With these words the little man abruptly put his spurs to his horse and rode swiftly away.

Josiah watched him disappear over the crest of the ridge. "That was strange," he told the mare. "He seemed quite friendly until I mentioned the Castle of Hope." Puzzling over the mysterious response of the gaudily dressed stranger, the prince rode on.

Moments later the mare topped a grassy rise and Josiah

reined her to a halt. In the valley before him stood a tall limestone promontory; atop it stood the partially finished walls of a castle. The young prince knew that he was getting his first glimpse of the Castle of Hope. He started forward slowly, surveying the castle as he rode.

Approaching from the south, Prince Josiah could see that the outer curtain wall of the Castle of Hope was only partially finished. The north wall appeared to be nearly complete while the east and west walls were only a few feet high. The south wall was hardly started. Josiah circled the mare to the north side of the castle, tied her to a small sycamore, and then approached the castle on foot.

With heavy heart he walked up the castle approach. Several logs had been placed as a temporary bridge across the moat, allowing him easy access. Pausing in the opening where one day the massive front gates would stand, he surveyed the structure. Work had started on the northeast and northwest towers of the outer curtain, but the other towers, gatehouses and gates were not even begun. The locations of the inner curtain and the buildings within were clearly marked, but not a bit of work had been done on them.

Hearing voices, he turned toward the sound. Two stone masons were atop the center section of the west wall busily laying a course of stone. Two youth were assisting by carrying mortar and stone to the top of the scaffolding. Josiah approached them. "Where might I find Master James?" he called.

The stone masons looked up from their work. Their faces registered surprise as they saw the young prince. "Master James, my lord? Here he comes now."

Josiah turned and saw a tall man striding through the gate opening.

"If I may be so bold as to ask, my lord," said one of the masons, "what brings you to the Castle of Hope?"

"His Majesty has sent me to help in the building of the castle," Josiah replied, and saw the two men glance at each other in surprise.

"Welcome to the Castle of Hope, my lord," a deep voice boomed, and Josiah turned to see the tall man approaching. "I am James of Arwyn, chief engineer on the castle project."

"I am Josiah of the Castle of Faith. His Majesty has sent me to assist you in the building of the castle."

"Praise the name of Emmanuel!" the tall man exulted. "Encouragement told me that you would come, though I had hardly dared to hope for such assistance." In his exuberance, he hugged Josiah. "Thank you for coming, my prince."

"How may I be of assistance, Master James?" the young prince asked.

"You have had a long ride, my lord. Allow me to care for your horse and get you something by way of refreshment, and then we shall talk."

Twenty minutes later, Prince Josiah and Master James sat on a huge boulder overlooking the castle and the village. "You have been told of our plight, I am sure," the engineer began.

Josiah nodded.

"The work started well enough," Master James continued. "The villagers pitched in willingly and the castle was progressing nicely. There was excitement among the workers. We had tremendous unity. The people realized that they were building for Emmanuel, and they were thrilled to have a part in his kingdom." He sighed heavily. "And then the first golden lamp was found and things have not been the same since."

"I have heard of the golden lamps," Josiah replied. He looked searchingly at the engineer. "What would you like for me to do? I am here to assist in any way that I can."

"As you know, most of the villagers and most of my staff have abandoned the work on the Castle of Hope in order to seek the golden lamps," James replied soberly. "Those few that remained faithful to King Emmanuel have continued to build, though they are very disheartened. Of a truth, I myself am disheartened. Prince Josiah, I am beginning to doubt that the Castle of Hope will ever be finished. I know that the project is Emmanuel's, but the work is proceeding so slowly that I often despair of seeing it completed."

He looked imploringly at the young prince. "Is there anything you can do to renew the interest of the people in the building of the castle? I have reminded them that this is His Majesty's castle, that the work will bring lasting rewards, and that any gain brought by the golden lamps is only temporary. So far, my words have fallen on deaf ears."

"How many remain loyal to the task?"

"Just a few. There is Paul the woodsman, who also now serves as the village reeve. He devotes his days to the castle. Then there is Phillip the huntsman, and his younger brother, Andrew. Phillip contributes to the castle project by providing us with venison."

"Is he a tall youth with dark hair?" Josiah asked.

James looked at him in surprise. "Aye. Do you know him?"

Josiah shook his head. "Nay, but I feel that I have already met him."

"Thomas and Marcella and their children work on the castle every day. They lost their son Michael in the attack on the village, and they are committed to the task of building the castle."

The young prince nodded. "Any others?"

"Very few. There are five or six others who stop in from time to time to work an hour here or an hour there, but their hearts are not really in it. And there are always a few children. To be honest, for the most part the people of the village have abandoned the castle."

A look of determination crossed the engineer's face. "I will ask Paul to call a town meeting tonight. You shall meet the villagers for yourself. Prince Josiah, if there is anything you can do to help us, I implore you to do it. The village needs this castle."

Chapter Fourteen

"And so Prince Josiah has been sent by King Emmanuel to assist us in the building of the Castle of Hope," Master James told the assembled villagers. "Please welcome the prince to Mitspah."

A few of the villagers smiled and gave nods of welcome, but most simply sat staring sullenly at Josiah. Nervously, the young prince stood to his feet. A cold night wind swept down from the mountainside, rustling the leaves on the trees and creating an atmosphere of restlessness.

"Greetings in the name of His Majesty, King Emmanuel," Josiah began, raising his voice to be heard by the townspeople. "Thank you, Master James, and thank you, Paul, for allowing me to address this assembly."

Josiah paused and looked across the audience. Most of the villagers sat quietly, arms folded across their chests, looking apathetically at him. A few seemed interested in what he had to say, while others seemed outright hostile. The young prince noticed that there were a large number of children and youth present. He cleared his throat.

"As you know, Emmanuel created the kingdom of Terrestria with you and me in mind. He then created us that we might love and honor him and that he might extend his great love to us. His love to us is unsearchable, everlasting, and greater than you or I will ever know. King Emmanuel wants the very best for the village of Mitspah, and for your children. As you remember, His Majesty commissioned the building of the Castle of Hope in order that you and your families might be safe from the attacks of Argamor and his knights."

Josiah turned and glanced toward the castle. Silver beams from the rising moon illuminated the east side of the walls while the western side was in darkness, giving the structure an eerie, unearthly appearance. He took a deep breath.

"I need not remind you that our adversary Argamor seeks to destroy us. He seeks to destroy your families, your children, your very lives. Good people of Mitspah, I know Argamor well, and I tell you the truth when I say that his every thought toward you is one of treachery and malice.

"I understand that just a few months ago a band of Argamor's dark knights attacked your village. In that attack, two of your number were killed and a young child was nearly taken captive. This incident is but a foreshadowing of what is to come. Please believe me when I say that there will be other attacks; the attack that took place is merely the first in a series of vicious attacks that our adversary has planned for this village."

The young prince paused and scanned his audience. The villagers sat quietly. Every eye was upon him, and it seemed that they were listening intently. Josiah looked up to see a snowy white dove perched in the branches of an ash tree. "Guide my words, I ask," he whispered.

"I have been, and will continue to do so," the dove replied in a quiet, gentle voice.

"I am told that the work on the Castle of Hope went very well until the first of the golden lamps was discovered," Josiah continued, addressing the townspeople. "Master James told me that you came together as one to build the castle; that you worked willingly; that you threw your heart and soul into this project for King Emmanuel. In fact, he told me that you exceeded his expectations."

Josiah sighed. "All that changed with the discovery of the first golden lamp. As we all know, work on the castle has nearly come to a standstill. The outer curtain has not been completed and work on the gates and gatehouses has not even started. The drawbridge has not been built, the towers are not completed, and the inner curtain is but a dream. A few still build faithfully every day, but I am told that most of the residents of the village are busy with other pursuits. Good people of Mitspah, if Argamor were to attack tonight, you would have no place of refuge for yourselves or your little ones."

"The Castle of Hope is a wonderful idea, my lord," one villager spoke up, "but we are busy with other matters. We have businesses to manage and families to provide for. We simply cannot spend every moment of every day working on the castle."

"His Majesty has not asked that you give every moment of every day," the young prince replied. "He knows that you have needs, and that you must provide for your families. When you first started building, the Castle of Hope was a priority to most of you. You were excited about building and you were willing to sacrifice to see the castle completed. All that has changed since Demas found the first golden lamp."

He took a deep breath. "Good people of Mitspah, the golden lamps are enchanting. They are beautiful to look at and quite exhilarating to hold. Ownership of a lamp must be an indescribable thrill. But may I remind you, any gain brought to you or to the village by the lamps is only temporal gain—every one of the beautiful horses which you are buying and the magnificent houses you are now building will stay right here when you and I are called to the Golden City of the Redeemed.

"On the other hand, every moment spent in the service of King Emmanuel will bring rewards that will endure forever, rewards that will go with you to the Golden City. The Castle of Hope was commissioned by His Majesty; when you work on the castle, you are earning rewards that will last forever."

The villagers sat quietly staring at Josiah. The young prince studied their somber faces as he tried his best to tell what they were thinking. Were his words having any impact at all?

Josiah reached within his doublet and withdrew the book, opening and displaying it before the villagers. "I am told that many of you are not properly armed; that you do not have His Majesty's sword. Good people, you must be armed and prepared for the next attack by Argamor's forces. Emmanuel is sending weapons for each of you, men and women alike, and they will arrive within the week."

He swung the book in a sweeping arc, transforming it into a glistening sword. Many of the villagers started, taken by surprise at the sudden appearance of the weapon. "Once the swords arrive, I will be happy to instruct any and all of you in their proper use." He glanced at Paul. "Perhaps we can schedule regular periods of training for all who wish to participate."

Paul nodded.

The young prince took a deep breath and then slowly scanned his audience. "Good people of Mitspah, are we in this together? Are you ready once again to throw yourselves heart and soul into the building of the Castle of Hope? Are you ready to finish this project for the honor and glory of King Emmanuel?"

The villagers sat quietly. No one moved. Josiah waited, but

there was no response.

"How many of you will be in your places on the work crews tomorrow?"

Josiah watched in consternation as only eight hands were raised. "Is that all? Do none of the rest of you intend to do your part to see the castle completed?"

The villagers sat silently. Tension filled the air.

"Perhaps I made a mistake in coming," the young prince said quietly. "I was sent to assist you in the building of the Castle of Hope, but I cannot help if you have no desire to see it completed." He looked at Paul. "Would you take charge of this meeting, sir? It seems that I am finished here."

Josiah was deeply troubled as he made his way down the narrow street, intending to take a walk on the hillside overlooking the little village. *His Majesty sent me,* he told himself, *so I made no mistake in coming, but I cannot help these people if they do not want help. How can I motivate an entire village to serve Emmanuel if their hearts are set on pursuing the golden lamps?*

"Wait, my lord!" a quiet voice called, and the young prince turned to see a young peasant about his age hurrying to catch up with him. Josiah waited.

"My lord, your coming to the village of Mitspah was no mistake," the youth blurted breathlessly as he approached. "The village needs the castle, needs it desperately, and yet, most of our people pursue the golden lamps instead of finishing the castle. Perhaps you are the one who can get us back to the task to which King Emmanuel has assigned us."

He took a deep breath and extended his hand. "I am Phillip, my lord. Please excuse my rash behavior in addressing you in this manner."

Josiah shook the hand that was offered. "Phillip the huntsman?"

Phillip's face registered his surprise. "Aye, that is my calling, my lord. Master James has assigned me the task of providing venison for his staff and for the workers. But how did you know?"

Josiah shrugged. "I have heard of you. You are said to be an archer of great skill."

The look of astonishment lingered on the young huntsman's face. "My lord, you are generous with your words. I am amazed that you knew my name." He stepped closer. "My lord, we do need you here. The Castle of Hope will not be built unless we have your help." In his exuberance, he seized Josiah's arm, and then, realizing what he had done, released his grip and stepped back in embarrassment. "A thousand pardons, my lord. I...I sometimes forget myself."

The young prince smiled. "Do not worry; it is of no consequence."

"The village does need the Castle of Hope, my lord," Phillip repeated eagerly, "and we do need your help in building it."

Josiah was immediately drawn to Phillip, realizing that the young huntsman shared his zeal to serve Emmanuel. "His Majesty sent me for that purpose, Phillip, and yet I do not know how to go about motivating your people to return to the castle project." He gestured toward the hillside before them. "Would you care to accompany me on a stroll?"

"Certainly, my lord."

The young prince laughed. "Would you do me a favor, Phillip?"

"Name it, my lord."

"Would you kindly cease calling me 'my lord' and address me by name? My name is Josiah."

"Certainly, my..." Phillip stopped, embarrassed. "Certainly, Josiah."

Both young men laughed.

Prince Josiah strode up the darkened slope toward the quarry and Phillip fell in step beside him. "Eight people volunteered to join the work crews tomorrow," the young prince observed soberly. "Are there really that few involved in the building of the castle?"

Phillip nodded. "Aye, that's about right. Apathy seems to be a way of life in Mitspah now that we have found the lamps."

Josiah turned and looked him in the eye. "Are you involved in the construction? Is the castle a priority to you? Is your heart yielded to Emmanuel?"

"I serve every day by providing Master James' staff and the work crews with venison. Many a day I hunt from sunup till sundown and I usually set aside my other work to do so. Were I not assigned to the hunt, you would find me building each day on the walls. Aye, my heart is yielded."

"I do not know you, yet already I feel a bond between us," Josiah said in response, "and somehow I came to expect such an answer. If your heart is yielded as you say it is, perhaps you can help me."

"In any way I can," Phillip replied fervently.

"Tell me how to restore the zeal that your people once had for the Castle of Hope. What can I say to encourage them to resume building? What can I do to cause them to see that the golden lamps have no lasting value, and that service to Emmanuel is of far greater importance than acquiring riches that will be lost the moment they head for the Golden City of the Redeemed?"

Phillip sighed. "If I knew, Josiah, I would have already said or done it. My heart is grieved that my fellow villagers have placed more value on the lamps than on service to our King. Nay, I really do not know what can be said or done."

The two walked in silence for several moments until Phillip reached out and touched Josiah on the arm. "We are approaching the quarry."

Josiah stopped. "The quarry from which the lamps were taken?"

Phillip nodded. "It's just over this next rise."

"Then let us not go any closer," the young prince replied. He dropped to a seat on a large boulder and his companion joined him.

"Have you lived in Mitspah all your life?" Josiah asked, studying the town and the partially completed castle in the light of the moon.

"I was born here," Phillip told him. "My father was an expert archer in the army of Emmanuel, and he also was born here. He died in the service of our King."

"Tell me about him," Josiah said quietly.

As the young prince listened, the young huntsman told of his father's great love for his King, of his delight in serving, and of his untimely death. "No one has ever loved Emmanuel more than my father did," he stated. "He lived and breathed for the opportunity to serve our King." He paused. "My desire is to be just like him."

Phillip went on to tell of the years of hardship following the death of his father and how he had managed to support his family. His eyes grew bright as he began to talk of his love for Rebecca and of his hopes of one day claiming her as his bride.

"She sounds lovely," Josiah observed.

"Aye, that she is," Phillip replied. "She's the most beautiful creature in all of Terrestria!"

Josiah laughed. "Is her heart yielded to Emmanuel, as yours is?"

The other nodded. "Aye. You would find her every day assisting in building the castle, except that her father won't allow it."

"Won't allow it? And why not?"

"Her father is Demas the merchant. He found the first of the golden lamps."

"And he has no interest in serving Emmanuel."

"Aye."

"Has he acquired wealth and possessions since finding the lamp?"

"He is now the wealthiest man in the village," Phillip replied. He turned and pointed. "Do you see the tallest of the houses being built on the ridge? That is the one belonging to Demas."

"Has he given permission for you to wed Rebecca?"

"I have not asked him." Phillip grinned. "But I think he knows that it is coming."

"And what will he say when you do ask?" Josiah queried.

"I would hope that he will grant permission," Phillip said slowly.

Josiah studied the village in silence for several long moments and Phillip sat quietly, realizing that his new friend was deep in thought. At last, Josiah spoke. "I shall attempt to talk to your people tomorrow," he said quietly. "Not in a group as we had tonight, but face to face, one by one. I shall ask them questions. Perhaps I shall be able to get inside their minds and hearts, to discover what they are thinking."

He gazed at the moonlit castle in the distance. "The Castle of Hope must be built."

Phillip abruptly caught his breath. "Josiah! Look!" He pointed downhill.

The young prince gazed intently in the direction that his

new friend indicated, but could see nothing out of the ordinary. "What is it? What do you see?"

"The golden hart!" Phillip was so agitated that he was trembling.

"A golden hart?"

"Its pelt has an unusual color and sheen to it," Phillip explained. "The fur almost looks as if it were made of spun gold." He pointed again. "Look, it's less than a hundred paces from us. You can see the moonlight reflecting from its antlers."

Josiah peered intently into the darkness. "I still don't see it."

"That's the largest hart I have ever seen," Phillip told him breathlessly. "I have pursued that wretched animal every day for more than a fortnight, but somehow I cannot kill it. On one occasion I dropped it, removed my arrow from its side, and went to get my horse to haul it out of the forest. When I returned, the hart was gone."

"It got up and walked away?"

Phillip shrugged. "Apparently. There were two other times when I put an arrow right through it without hitting it. I'm beginning to think that the animal is not really there—that it's just an apparition of some sort. And yet, there it is, right now. I can see it!"

Josiah was still studying the hillside below. "I still don't see it."

"Do you think I am mad if I can see something and you cannot?"

The young prince shook his head. "I'm not sure what to think."

"One day I will get that hart and bring him back to the village draped over the back of my saddle," Phillip vowed. "One day, the golden hart will be mine."

Chapter Fifteen

"I'm a busy man, my lord," the tall farmer puffed as he forked down hay from the loft, "and I really don't have time to talk. Once my cow is fed and milked, I'm off to the quarry. There are more golden lamps to be had, you know, and I might as well have one as the next fellow."

"Then I won't detain you," Prince Josiah promised. "I just want to ask you a couple of questions and I'll be out of your way before the cow is milked. As a matter of fact, I'll start the milking for you." He grabbed the stool and a milk bucket and approached the black-and-white cow, which stood swishing its tail nervously.

"Fair enough," the man grunted.

Josiah scooted the bucket under the cow and began milking. "I am told that when the castle project began, Master James assigned the people of Mitspah to various work crews," he told the farmer. "To what work crew were you assigned?"

"I don't know that it matters now," the man replied, "but I was assigned to work with the stone masons. We were building the north curtain wall."

"Not much is being done on the castle now," the young prince observed. "The north curtain is not even finished."

The man shrugged as he made his way down from the loft. "There are hundreds of people living in this town, my lord. Is it my responsibility to see that the castle is built?"

Josiah's hands flew. The white jets of milk beat a steady rhythm against the bottom of the milk bucket. The farmer paused to watch and his eyes widened in surprise. "Say, you're quite an accomplished milker! Not many princes know how to do that, I reckon."

Josiah laughed. "I've done a lot of things that most princes haven't, I would imagine." He turned from the bucket. "Care to finish?"

"You're faster than me," the farmer replied with a chuckle. "I'll just watch."

"If I may ask you a personal question, sire," Josiah ventured, continuing to milk furiously as he talked, "why did you stop working on the Castle of Hope?"

The man shrugged. "I think you know the answer, my lord. Why should I slave away at the castle while others are finding the golden lamps and achieving the prosperity that comes with them? If there are other lamps to be had—and I'm sure there are, for legend says there are forty—then I want my share of the wealth. That's only fair."

"The Castle of Hope was commissioned by His Majesty," Josiah reminded the man. "Any work you do on the castle is service done for Emmanuel."

"I'm doing this for my family, my lord. I want my wife and children to have as good a life as anyone else in the village. I want my wife to have a nice house and beautiful clothes. I want my children to have a better life than I did as a child."

"What if you lose your family in the process?" Josiah asked quietly.

"Lose my family?" A look of agitation spread across the

man's countenance. "How could I lose my family by going to the quarry and seeking to find a golden lamp?"

"Well, for one thing, you're teaching your children that prosperity is more important than the King's business. But not only that, once completed, the Castle of Hope will be a place of safety for your family when Argamor's forces attack. If he should attack this afternoon, what would happen to your family?"

"The attack was an isolated incident. Hopefully, it will never happen again."

"I too would like to hope for that, sire, but I know Argamor too well. He will attack again, and the village must be ready. The castle must be built."

The milk pail was now full and Josiah lifted it from beneath the cow. "Do you have another?"

"Nay, but I'll empty this up at the house and finish the milking myself," the farmer replied, reaching for the bucket. "Good day, my lord."

"Sire, think about your family," the young prince said soberly, as he headed for the door of the little cow shed, "and think about the need for the castle. The King's business should always come before our own personal gain."

"Once I find my own golden lamp I'll return to the work crew immediately," the farmer replied sincerely, "and that's a promise. Good day, my lord."

Josiah was deep in thought as he strolled down the narrow lane. *None of the villagers are opposed to the building of the castle,* he told himself, *but they don't see it as a priority in their own lives. Somehow they don't see the importance of having a place of safety when the enemy attacks again. How can I help them see what is at stake here? How can I help them develop a sense of urgency for the completion of the castle?*

He looked up to see a young couple approaching. The man carried a well-worn mattock and the woman carried a long wooden pike with a sharp iron point. "Good day, good people of Mitspah," he greeted them.

"Good day to you, my lord," they both replied pleasantly.

"Are you on your way to the Castle of Hope?" the young prince inquired. "I see that you have work tools."

The man snorted derisively. "We're working in the quarry, sire, but it has nothing to do with that wretched castle. Nay, it's golden lamps we're after."

Josiah sighed. "The Castle of Hope was commissioned by His Majesty," he reminded them, "and yet at present it stands incomplete, useless as a defense against the enemy. Why not do your part to see it finished for the glory of our King?"

"If our King wants the castle built, then let him send workers to build it. The wife and I have better things to do."

"By that you mean search for the golden lamps."

"Exactly," the man replied, stepping around Josiah. "Now, if you'll excuse us, my lord, we really must be on our way. Good day, my lord."

"Good day, sir," Josiah replied slowly.

He decided to visit the quarry and see for himself the source of the golden lamps. As he followed the well-worn path up the slope from the village he was joined by a slender man with a friendly smile. "Good day to you, my lord," the man greeted him cheerfully. "Lovely day, is it not?"

"Good day to you, sire. Indeed, it is a lovely day."

"I am Barnabas," the man introduced himself, "and you are the young prince sent by King Emmanuel, I believe."

"Aye, sire, I am Josiah," the young prince replied. "Barnabas. Weren't you one of the first ones to find a golden lamp?"

"Actually, I was the second fortunate to find a lamp," the

man replied with a huge smile, though not boastfully. "Thus far thirteen of those magnificent vessels have been discovered." He pointed. "Do you see the second house on the ridge, my lord? That is the one I am building."

As they strolled along it suddenly occurred to Josiah that the man was heading in the same direction he was. "Are you also going to the quarry, sir?"

"Aye," Barnabas replied with another huge smile. "Perhaps fortune will smile on me a second time, eh? Perhaps I may find a second golden lamp."

Stunned, Josiah stopped in the middle of the trail. "A second lamp, sir? You seek a second lamp?"

The man's smile grew, and a strange light played in his eyes. "Ah, yes! Would it not be splendid if I were to find a second lamp?"

"But you already have one, sir! I have been told that you have become a very wealthy man—that you want for nothing. Why would you desire to find a second lamp?"

Barnabas stopped and looked at Josiah and a mystified look crossed his face. "My lord, look at what the first lamp has done for me. As you said, I now want for nothing. We are building one of the most magnificent houses in all of Terrestria. My wife now wears clothing that previously she could only dream of. I have horses, and servants, and vast amounts of gold and silver. Aye, the golden lamp has been good to me! My lord, I now have everything I need, everything I've ever wanted."

"But if you have everything you need and want, why do you desire another golden lamp?"

The man stared at Josiah as if he could not comprehend the question. "The lamp has brought me tremendous wealth and numerous possessions. Why would I not desire another?"

"But is not one lamp enough?"

"How could one lamp ever be enough, my lord?" The man

smiled broadly and the strange light once again played in his eyes. "Oh, that I could find a hundred golden lamps! Oh, that I could find a thousand!"

"What about the Castle of Hope, sir?"

The man turned to stare at him and the smile vanished from his countenance. "What about it?"

"His Majesty commissioned us to build it, and yet, the castle stands incomplete, a mockery to the name of our King. The outer curtain is not even completed. Work has not even started on the drawbridge and gates and gatehouses. Does that not concern you?"

A strange smile played on Barnabas' lips. "Why should the castle concern me, my lord? My family and I don't need it. We have our wealth." He glanced toward the quarry and then back to Josiah. "Excuse me, my lord, but I really must be going. I'm on a quest for another lamp, you know. Good day."

"Good day, sir," the young prince said slowly as Barnabas hurried up the path.

"Ready for another day of working on the castle?" Andrew asked eagerly, as Nathaniel answered his knock. "We should finish the north wall today."

"I—I'm not going today," his friend replied, opening the cottage door a little wider.

"Not going?" Andrew was puzzled. "Why not?"

Nathaniel wouldn't look at him. "I—I'm going to the quarry."

"The quarry? To search for a golden lamp?"

"Aye."

Andrew was stunned. "Nathaniel, what about the castle? Building the castle is the King's work, and we both agreed that it's far more important than searching for a golden lamp!"

His friend sighed. "I know, Andrew, but—well, sometimes it seems like everyone else is going to find a golden lamp but us. If I can find a lamp I can help my family. You know we need the money. And what about your family? Imagine how pleased your mother would be if you could hand her a golden lamp and know that she would never again have another need! Wouldn't that be grand?"

"Aye, it would," Andrew agreed, "but how could I stand before Emmanuel, knowing that I had put my own interests ahead of his work? I just can't do that, Nathaniel."

"Come with me just this one day," Nathaniel argued. "Let's go to the quarry today, and tomorrow we'll go back to work on the castle."

Andrew shook his head. "I can't do it. The castle is King Emmanuel's, and it has to come first."

Nathaniel shrugged. "Then I'll see you this evening."

Andrew nodded and walked away, keenly disappointed with the decision that his friend had made. *Is all of Mitspah going to abandon the castle?* he thought sadly. *Even Nathaniel now places more value on the golden lamps than on service to our King. Are the lamps more important than the King's work?*

Josiah spent most of the morning attempting to talk with individual villagers, but the response was always the same: the people simply were no longer interested in building the Castle of Hope. Each person that the young prince talked with expressed one burning desire—to find a golden lamp and begin to acquire riches as other villagers had done.

Disheartened by the response of the villagers, Prince Josiah decided to visit the castle site and again view the builders' progress. He strolled back down the hill, passed through the nearly deserted village, and then approached the castle. Master James and two stone masons were hard at work on top of the north curtain wall, and a couple of youth were serving as stone and mortar carriers, but otherwise, the castle was nearly deserted.

As he walked up the approach ramp and crossed the logs that served as a temporary drawbridge, a voice hailed him. "Prince Josiah! Welcome to the Castle of Hope, my lord."

Josiah turned. Twenty paces away, a stocky man with a red beard was mixing mortar in a large, flat wooden box on the ground.

"Welcome to the castle, my lord," the man repeated as Josiah approached. "I'm Mark, chief mortar mixer for the castle project." He grinned ruefully. "Actually, I'm the only mortar mixer left on this project. It seems that everyone else has deserted."

"Good morning, sir," Josiah replied cheerfully. He stood for a long moment gazing at the castle walls. "There's still a long way to go, isn't there?" he observed quietly.

Mark nodded. "The work started well enough. The entire village pitched in and worked together and the walls went up with record speed." He sighed. "Everything changed when the first of the golden lamps was found, though. Now it seems that almost no one is willing to work on the castle."

"I appreciate your willingness to work, though, sir," Josiah told him fervently, "and we both know that King Emmanuel is pleased. Your labor will be rewarded."

A pained expression appeared on Mark's face. "I wish you hadn't said that, my lord."

Josiah was puzzled. "Why, sir?"

The mortar mixer sighed. "Today is my last day to serve at

the castle." He looked at the ground as he said the words.

The young prince grabbed the man by the arms. "Why, Mark? Why is this your last day?"

The man sighed again. "There's no hiding it, I suppose, so I might as well out and tell you. Tomorrow I plan to go to the quarry and search for a golden lamp of my own."

Josiah's heart sank. "You...you plan to quit? Right in the middle of the project? They need you, sir!"

Mark wouldn't look at him. "I know, my lord, but—" He glanced up at Josiah and then down at the ground again. "My wife has been after me to leave the castle and find a lamp for us. She's seen some of the other women in the village whose husbands have found lamps and become prosperous and she wants what they have."

He sighed. "I suppose I can't really blame her. It is a bit disheartening to work up here on the castle while most of the rest of the village searches for the golden lamps. I too would like to get ahead in life as some others are doing. I'd like to build a beautiful home for my wife, buy a nice horse or two, provide a few nice possessions for my children, just as the others have. It's the Terrestrian dream."

Prince Josiah shook his head sadly. "Don't trade that which is forever for that which will be taken from you in a moment. Don't trade King Emmanuel's blessings for mere possessions. The golden lamps glisten enchantingly, sir, but not one of them will be carried to the Golden City of the Redeemed. Good day, Mark."

Four young girls sat in the shade of a huge oak, giggling with glee as they playfully tossed acorns at each other. Above their heads, a frisky squirrel leaped from branch to branch in one death-defying leap after another, each time scrambling frantically to keep from falling. The girls laughed at his antics. The furry little creature saw the girls and hurriedly scampered up the trunk of the tree.

Diana gazed longingly down at the quarry, which swarmed with activity. "I wish Papa could find a golden lamp like your father did," she sighed wistfully to Mira, "and then perhaps our family could have nice things like yours. Perhaps I could even get a pony!"

"Don't we all wish that," another girl, Deborah, replied. "It doesn't seem fair that just a few families should find a lamp and have all that money and happiness while other families do without."

"Finding the lamp hasn't really brought happiness to our family," Mira said thoughtfully.

"We all know better than that," Deborah snapped at her. "Your father has all that gold, and he's building that magnificent house and your mother has all those nice clothes and things and... and what about your pony? You can't tell me that you haven't enjoyed owning that pony!" She clenched her fingers and rolled her eyes. "I'd give anything to have a pony like yours!"

Mira sighed. "Aye, it is true, I have enjoyed having the pony," she replied. "But finding the golden lamp and getting nice things hasn't really helped our family. Father is now so busy that he doesn't even have time to talk to me! And Mother—Mother has become a different person. All she ever thinks about now is getting even more gold and having even more nice things! I almost feel—" She stopped abruptly, biting her lip as if to keep from crying.

"Almost feel what?" Diana prompted.

Mira hesitated. "I almost feel as though I no longer have a mother and father," she said quietly. "The golden lamp has changed them both. I wish—I wish that Father had never found the lamp in the first place!"

The other girls were silent.

Josiah walked up one of the wooden ramps and stood atop the north curtain, gazing across the village of Mitspah. Master James spotted him and hurried over. "Prince Josiah! It's an honor to have you here, my lord."

"Good morning, Master James," Josiah replied absently. "And how is the work progressing today?"

"There's been another attack on the castle, I'm afraid," the engineer replied. "Many of our tools are missing, and the scaffolding along the west wall was badly damaged."

"Last night?"

Master James nodded. "Apparently." He frowned. "I really have no idea who could be responsible, or how he is able to accomplish such treachery. Two of my most trusted men were on guard detail last night."

He laughed. "Well, enough of my troubles." He studied Josiah. "You are troubled, Prince Josiah; I saw it on your face as you approached. What is wrong?"

The young prince was silent for a long moment. "I was sent by His Majesty to help you in the building of the castle," he began. "I came expecting to challenge your people, renew their vision to build the castle, and then build with them as they took up the project with renewed zeal. Alas, it is not happening as I had envisioned. I have talked with a number of your people, both last night and today, and it seems that their attitudes can be summed up in one word: apathy. They simply don't care if the castle is ever completed. It's as though the golden lamps have taken control of their minds and hearts."

Master James nodded. "That's exactly what the old man said would happen."

"The old man?"

"An old man appeared just moments after Demas found the first lamp. He warned Demas and the others that the lamp would attempt to control the one who possessed it."

"The lamps are doing more than that," Josiah observed. "It seems that they now have the power to control even those who have not found one." He nodded down toward the man mixing mortar. "Even Mark plans to desert the castle project. Today is his last day."

"Do you have any suggestions, my lord?"

Josiah shook his head. "I have no idea what to do. Right now I simply plan to go up on the hillside above the quarry and send another petition to the Golden City. Perhaps Emmanuel has further instructions for us."

"Thank you for coming," Master James said quietly. "Your presence has been a real encouragement to me."

Josiah nodded and walked away.

Phillip returned from the day's hunt to find Andrew waiting for him outside the village wall. "Phillip, may I talk with you?"

"Aye, of course," the young huntsman replied, reining the mare to stop beside his brother. "What's on your mind?"

"Are we really making the right choice? I sometimes wonder if—Phillip, what if everyone finds a golden lamp except our family?"

Phillip dismounted. "Andrew, we're serving King Emmanuel! He's the one who commissioned the building of the castle. This is his work, and we must be faithful to do as he has told us."

Andrew sighed. "I know, but—" He paused, struggling with

the words, and his brother waited patiently. "I watch Mama when she passes some of the women whose husbands have found lamps. I watch her eyes as she looks at their fine clothing, and...and there's sadness there, Phillip. I know Mama would like to have fine new clothing and nice things like they do. Would it be wrong to go to the quarry and search for a lamp to buy nice things for Mama?"

Phillip put a hand on his shoulder. "Keep working faithfully at the castle, little brother, and I'll keep hunting faithfully, just as I have been assigned. Mama would rather that we stay faithful to serve our King, rather than to abandon his work in hopes of getting nice things for her."

Andrew looked up, and his eyes revealed his uncertainty. "Are you sure?"

Phillip nodded confidently. "Aye, I know it!"

The younger brother sighed heavily. "I know in my heart that what you're saying is right, but I guess I just needed to hear you say it. I want to stay faithful to King Emmanuel, but sometimes I find that my heart is drawn to other things."

The moon slipped silently over the kingdom of Terrestria as the young prince huddled miserably on a rocky ledge high above the Castle of Hope. He could see the flickering glow of cooking fires in the village far below and knew that most of the villagers were preparing for the evening meal. But even at this late hour a muffled cacophony of sounds still issued from the direction of the quarry and he knew that a number of villagers still labored by the feeble light of lanterns and torches, hoping desperately to find another golden lamp.

He shook his head. What was the term Phillip had used when describing the practice of searching in the darkness rather than returning to one's home for rest and nourishment? *Overtime.* That was it.

He watched the stars as they came to life one by one. He smiled. Two of Emmanuel's constellations were clearly visible from this vantage point.

He sighed. He had sent not one but four separate petitions to the Golden City during the long afternoon as he pondered his predicament. Why didn't King Emmanuel answer?

Sensing that he was not alone, he turned, and then jumped in fright. Standing less than five paces from him was the ethereal form of a woman. Tall and slender and dressed in a flowing white gown, the figure was so gossamer and transparent that he could still see the rocks and trees behind her. As he watched, the apparition became translucent, and then solid. The lady had a pleasant, friendly face framed softly by long, golden hair. Her pearl-white gown fluttered gently in the breeze. In her left hand she held a single rose, a deep crimson blossom that glowed with a light all its own.

Josiah's heart beat faster. "Lady Prudence!"

The white lady moved silently toward him. After a long moment, she spoke. "Prince Josiah, His Majesty knows that you are disheartened. He has sent me in answer to your petitions."

"I really don't know what to do," Josiah exclaimed with a heavy sigh. "The Castle of Hope sits abandoned, yet the people of Mitspah won't listen when I plead with them to finish the castle for His Majesty. Their hearts and minds have been captured by the allure of the golden lamps. The entire village seems possessed by the desire to find a lamp and acquire wealth."

He stood as Lady Prudence approached. "If only they could see the results of their choices, my lady! If only they could see what will happen if Argamor's forces attack again before the castle is completed. If only they could see that the golden lamps and every one of their glittering possessions will be lost the moment King Emmanuel calls them to the Golden City! If only they could see—"

"...the future," the white lady finished for him.

"Aye!" The young prince cried. "If only they could see the future!"

"Tonight they shall," the ethereal visitor said quietly.

Josiah turned toward her in bewilderment, not understanding the meaning of her words.

"Hasten back to the village," she instructed. "Have Paul call a meeting of all the men of the village one hour from now at the quarry. Every man must be present. Tonight the men of Mitspah shall visit the Lake of Destiny."

Chapter Sixteen

The moon darted behind the clouds as the men of the village trudged up the hill toward the quarry. Paul and Master James had built a huge bonfire to light their way. Within minutes, dozens of men were milling uncertainly at the edge of the excavation. "What's the meaning of this, Paul?" one man asked.

"We'll all find out when everyone is present," the tall reeve replied. "I myself do not know; I'm simply following orders."

Ten minutes later, every man in the village was present. Paul raised his voice and addressed the assembly. "Gather round, men. Move closer to the fire so that you might hear." Obligingly, the group huddled closer.

"Prince Josiah has asked us to assemble, gentlemen, so I now ask you to give him your attention. Prince Josiah, the men are at your disposal."

"As you know," Josiah began, raising his voice to be heard, "His Majesty sent me to challenge and encourage you to return to the construction of the Castle of Hope. I have already talked with many of you, but it seems that so far my words have fallen on deaf ears. Tonight, men, I shall make yet another plea."

Many of the men stirred impatiently. "I can't believe that he would call us up here at night for this," a low voice muttered.

"Hear me out," Josiah demanded. "Tonight, we shall take you into the future." Instantly, a hush fell over the entire crowd.

"Two dear friends of mine have agreed to assist us in making this journey." As Josiah said these words, two human figures began to materialize on the far side of the fire.

Men cried out in fear. Some turned to run.

"Hold your ground!" Josiah called. "For they are not spirits, as you suppose. These two have been sent by Emmanuel to enable each of you to see the consequences of your choices. I give you my two good friends, Lady Prudence and her brother, Sir Wisdom."

The men of Mitspah stood staring in astonishment as the two ethereal figures moved closer. Mouths dropped open; limbs trembled; faces were ashen. One man pointed at Sir Wisdom. "It's the old man," he stammered. "The one who warned us of the golden lamps!"

Sir Wisdom laughed. "Aye, you are correct," he replied.

Some of the men actually trembled in fright as Sir Wisdom spoke. "Tonight, good men of Mitspah, we shall take you to visit the future. Tonight we shall visit the Lake of Destiny that you might see the consequences of the choices that you are making. Lady Prudence, please call the lepidopteras."

The white lady raised her hand to her mouth and gave a loud, shrill whistle. The villagers simply stared at her in bewilderment.

Moments later they turned as one and gazed upward as peals of thunder echoed across the heavens. Josiah felt a surge of wonder as the familiar sound fell upon his ears; he knew what was about to take place.

"Look!" a man cried in utter astonishment. "What is it?"

Thunder rocked the hillside as the night sky pulsed with brilliant flashes of color and light. Dazzling beams of colored light shot across the heavens. Moments later, huge winged creatures filled the sky above the hillside. They hovered a hundred feet above the stunned group of villagers. Flashes of multi-colored light blazed from their enormous wings, illuminating the quarry.

"Butterflies!" one villager exclaimed in awe, when he finally found his voice. "Butterflies bigger than houses!"

"Look at the colors!"

"Look at the quarry! It's brighter than daytime!"

There were hundreds of the breath-taking creatures. Their shimmering, transparent wings beat in unison as they hovered, flashing dazzling rainbows of color and light. As they dropped slowly toward the earth, the downdraft from their gigantic wings made the branches of the trees on the hillside dance and shake as if they were being pounded by a violent windstorm.

As the men watched in amazement, the lepidopteras dropped from their hover and spiraled down to land noiselessly upon the grass. Instantly the thunder of their wings ceased and silence prevailed. Once on the ground, the magnificent creatures slowly opened and closed their huge, iridescent wings repeatedly.

"The lepidopteras have come to transport you to the Lake of Destiny," Sir Wisdom told the men. "Have no fear; these beautiful creatures are the servants of King Emmanuel and will do you no harm. Each of you is to climb upon the back of a lepidoptera, which will then carry you to the lake. Lady Prudence and I will await you there."

With these words, the two ethereal visitors vanished from sight.

The men looked at one another uncertainly.

One man voiced his reluctance. "Does he really expect that

we'll get on the backs of these things?"

"I don't think I will," another said.

"I'm not about to," declared a third.

Prince Josiah hurried forward. "You can trust the lepi-dopteras," he announced. "As Sir Wisdom told you, they have been sent by King Emmanuel. I myself have ridden the lepi-dopteras more than once. Here—I'll show you."

With these words, the young prince ran forward and leaped upward onto the abdomen of the nearest lepidoptera. He then crawled forward and sat on the thorax of the huge creature. Wrapping his legs around the lepidoptera's middle, he leaned forward and grasped the powerful muscles attaching the massive wings to the body.

The huge wings immediately began to beat rapidly and the lepidoptera lifted slowly into the air. The young prince felt a breathtaking surge of excitement. "Follow me!" he cried to the men on the ground, hoping that they could hear him above the noise of the mighty wings.

As he watched, one villager ran forward and scrambled onto the back of a lepidoptera. When he was safely in place, the huge winged creature lifted gently into the air. Moments later, another villager followed his example, and then another. Within moments, the rest of the men had climbed aboard the remaining lepidopteras and been lofted into the air.

The noise of the mighty wings increased as the entire band of huge butterflies began to climb higher. Josiah looked down and discovered that they were already several hundred feet above the village. He tightened his grip.

With giant wings beating in perfect unison, the band of lep-idopteras banked sharply to the left and began to fly directly west. Josiah relaxed and watched the reactions of the other men. Some of the men sat rigid with looks of terror on their faces, while others seemed to be concentrating on maintaining a good grip on their winged mounts. A few actually seemed to be enjoying the unusual ride.

After a ten-minute flight Josiah spotted a roaring fire on the ground below. The band of lepidopteras circled twice above the flames and then spiraled downward to land upon the grass less than a hundred paces from the fire. As Josiah climbed down from the back of his lepidoptera he saw the glistening waters of the Lake of Destiny. The moon had created a shimmering, silvery path across the surface of the water.

Of their own accord the men of the village scrambled down from the lepidopteras and hurried toward the fire. Lady Prudence and Sir Wisdom were waiting to greet them. "Men of Mitspah, tonight you shall..." Thunder drowned out Sir Wisdom's words as the mighty lepidopteras rose majestically into the air, and so the nobleman waited patiently. The men watched wordlessly as the mighty band of lepidopteras disappeared into the distant skies, accompanied by brilliant flashes of fiery colored light.

When silence prevailed Sir Wisdom spoke again. "Men of Mitspah, tonight you shall visit the future. Your future. If your heart is open, men, what you see tonight will change you forever."

The men of the village moved closer. Josiah was pleased to note that each man seemed interested and attentive. "What are we to do, my lord?" one man asked.

"Two paths lay ahead of you, gentlemen. You must choose wisely. If you would see what lies ahead, walk into the lake."

"Walk *into* the lake, my lord?"

"Aye," Sir Wisdom replied quietly. "The Lake of Destiny can show you what lies ahead for you, in order that you might choose the path that you would take. Look ahead in order that you may choose your path wisely."

The two ethereal visitors moved silently toward the water. The men found themselves compelled to follow.

Sir Wisdom paused at the water's edge, standing at the very point where the shimmering path began. "Follow the silver path. You need not fear the water; the lake itself will take you into the realm of what lies ahead in order that you might learn and profit."

The men of the village hesitated, looking at each other uncertainly. A loon called from across the lake, a lonely, mournful call that seemed to echo within one's soul. Prince Josiah stepped forward. "Follow me, gentlemen. There is nothing to fear. We are about to visit the future." With these words, he stepped into the lake.

Prince Josiah's heart was pounding furiously as he waded out into the rippling waters of the Lake of Destiny. The water swirled around his knees, but there was no sensation of cold wetness. He waded deeper. When the water reached his waist, he turned and called to the men on the bank reassuringly. "Do not fear, gentlemen. You are about to view the future as it could be. If your hearts are open, this night will change your lives forever."

The men on the bank hesitated.

"Do not be afraid," Josiah called to them. "Simply follow me into the lake."

Several men stepped into the waters and walked toward him. Paul was among them. He paused when the waters reached his knees and stared at the lake in astonishment. "I don't feel the water," he cried. "It's as if the water isn't really there." Turning to those who still hesitated on the bank, he called, "Come on in, fellows. You have to experience this!"

When he said this the other men almost immediately followed him into the water. Exclamations of amazement filled

the air as they too realized that they could not feel the sensations of cold water that they had expected.

"Stay with me, men, and we'll enter the future together,"
Josiah called. He stepped forward with a number of the men at
his side. The water grew deeper, reaching their shoulders, but
they pushed resolutely forward. Still they felt no sensation of
cold water around their bodies.

Several of the men gave small gasps of fear as the water
closed over their heads. They looked up to notice a shimmering, silvery ceiling just above their heads, and realized that
they were looking *up* at the *surface* of the lake. They were sub-
merged beneath the water! Awestruck to realize that they had
already passed beneath the surface of the lake, and yet still
could breathe, they began to laugh.

Josiah and the men saw a sudden flash of light. For just an
instant, the men felt dizzy and nauseous, and some of them
closed their eyes. They opened them to discover that their sur-
roundings had changed. Shading their eyes against the sudden
brightness that engulfed them, they looked around. They were
standing in the middle of a narrow trail that led through a
dense forest. Judging from the position of the sun, it seemed
that it was late afternoon.

One man glanced upward to notice that the shimmering
ceiling had disappeared and they were no longer beneath the
waters of the lake. "The lake is gone, fellows!" he cried in astonishment. "I think we've stepped through a doorway into
another world!"

"We are visitors into the realm of the future," Josiah told
his charges, "though we live in the realm of the present. The
people we are about to meet live in the realm of the future, so
they can neither see nor hear us, and there is nothing we can
do to influence them in any way. You may be surprised to meet

yourselves in a few moments, but remember, the people that you are about to see are future versions of yourselves.

"We are about to witness a spectacular battle, but do not be alarmed; none of us will come to any harm, and there is nothing any of us can do to change the outcome of the battle. We are merely spectators."

He looked the group over. "Is everyone here?"

"Demas and Barnabas are not here," a voice replied.

"Lucius is not here either," another man volunteered.

"Shall I go back for them?" Paul asked.

Josiah nodded. "Simply walk back the way we came and you will emerge from the lake."

Paul's face wore a determined look. "We'll be back in a moment," he promised. He walked back up the trail and then instantly vanished from sight. The villagers looked at each other in astonishment.

Moments later Paul reappeared with the three men.

"Follow me, gentlemen," the young prince said, stepping forward on the trail. "We are about to witness the future." The men followed close behind him in a tight cluster.

After a hike of a few minutes the trail opened up and the group found themselves on the side of a mountain overlooking a quiet valley. "Look!" one man exclaimed, pointing. "There's our village!"

"And there's the castle," another replied. "But look—it's finished!"

The Castle of Hope stood proudly atop the rocky promontory, white and glistening in the afternoon sun. Tall and stately, her towers stood like sentries keeping vigilant watch over the town. Her gates were massive. Royal purple banners flew proudly above each tower, each emblazoned with symbols of the cross and crown, King Emmanuel's own coat of arms.

The Castle of Hope was a magnificent picture of strength and safety.

"Incredible," one of the men breathed. "The castle is mighty impressive, isn't it?"

"I didn't realize that it would be that big or that magnificent," another remarked.

"This is the future," Prince Josiah reminded the men. "This is exactly what the Castle of Hope will look like once it is completed."

The villagers stood silent for several long moments as they admired the majestic beauty of the castle. "The wall around the village is completed," came the comment. "Notice how sturdy it looks."

"Let's move closer," Josiah suggested. The men followed him down the hillside and onto the road leading to the village. Moments later the sounds of hooves rang out and the group turned to see a handsome gray horse bearing down upon them. The group hurried to one side of the roadway.

"It's Demas!" one man shouted. "Demas, how are you?" The horseman sped by without answering.

"He couldn't see or hear us," Josiah reminded the group. "We are merely visitors from another realm of time."

"Was that really me?" Demas asked in utter astonishment.

"It was a future version of you," Josiah told him.

Just as Josiah and the group of men reached the front gates of the village, one of the men cried out in fear, "Look! Look behind us!"

The group turned as one. At that moment, a band of horseman appeared at the crest of a ridge and rode swiftly down upon the village. Even from such a distance Josiah could see that each rider wore dark armor. "Argamor's men!"

A long line of marching infantry approached from the south,

each knight arrayed in the dark armor of Argamor, their shields emblazoned with his coat of arms, the red dragon. A company of pike men in dark armor swept over the hills from the east. The banners fluttering in the breeze from the tip of each lance bore the same red dragon.

"The village is under attack!" Demas wailed.

"What shall we do?" Phillip asked Josiah. "I didn't even bring my longbow."

"We do nothing but watch," the young prince replied. "We are visitors from another time. There is nothing we can do to change the outcome of the battle."

In the village, a gong began to ring. Paul glanced up at the tower with an amused expression. "That's me. I'm sounding the alarm."

"Let's watch from the hillside," Josiah suggested, and the men followed him up the slope. Just as they took seats in the grass, a company of enemy archers emerged from the forest behind them.

In the valley below, the villagers were running for the safety of the castle. The reeve had already closed and barred the gates of the town wall. Archers took up positions on top of the wall. "Look," Josiah said to Phillip, "you're among them."

"We'll see what sort of archer I am, won't we?" Phillip replied with a grin. He leaned forward. "This will be interesting. I hope I do well."

"I hope we all do well."

As the men watched, the vast army of Argamor's dark knights converged on the village of Mitspah. Companies of archers atop the walls sent a barrage of arrows into the ranks of the enemy in an attempt to hold them at bay until the villagers had reached the safety of the castle. A score of dark knights produced a small battering ram and set to work on the city gates while a fusillade of arrows rained down upon them, killing some and wounding others. After losing a number of their comrades, the dark knights abandoned the battering ram and fell back.

Enemy troops with scaling ladders moved into position and placed their ladders against the village wall. Dark knights with swords drawn rushed up the ladders and gained access to the top of the wall. The archers drew swords and swiftly fought them back, completely clearing the walls.

"We haven't lost a single man," Paul commented, as he watched the battle in astonishment. "They've already lost scores of men."

"We fight with the weapons given to us by Emmanuel," Josiah replied. "Victory is assured when we battle in his might."

At that moment the villagers atop the wall hurriedly left their posts and retreated to the safety of the Castle of Hope. "What are they doing?" Barnabas inquired as the castle drawbridge went up. "Why did they leave the walls?"

"All the other villagers are safely within the castle," Josiah told him. "The archers have moved to the shelter of the castle for protection as they fight. The enemy are at a huge disadvantage when they attack the castle."

Scores of dark knights screaming with rage suddenly rushed forward and swarmed up the scaling ladders, taking possession of the village walls. They unbarred the gates and opened them. The remaining companies of evil forces flooded into Mitspah and rushed toward the castle.

Time stood still. Prince Josiah and the men with him watched in fascinated silence as they witnessed a spectacular battle for the Castle of Hope and the village of Mitspah. Wave after wave of dark knights assaulted the walls and gates of the castle time after time, only to be beaten back by determined villagers bearing the weapons of King Emmanuel. At last, an enemy trumpet sounded the call to retreat and the dark knights ran for the hills, leaving more than half their number lying dead in the streets of Mitspah.

The men on the hillside raised a lively cheer. "We have beaten them!" they exulted. "The village and the castle are safe! We have beaten the enemy!"

Prince Josiah gathered the men around him. "We have visited the future and witnessed that for which we came," he told them. "Let's head back to the present."

He led the men back into the forest and found the trail by which they had come. Still pondering the breathtaking battle they had just witnessed, the group retraced their steps. Moments later, as they followed the trail up a gentle slope, they looked up to see the shimmering silver surface just above their heads. As they climbed higher, they abruptly broke through the surface and found themselves emerging from the Lake of Destiny. The moon was now high overhead.

They stepped from the lake and walked across the sandy lakeshore, surprised to find that their clothing was not even wet. Two white forms moved in the darkness ahead. Sir Wisdom and Lady Prudence were waiting for them by the dying fire.

"Men of Mitspah," Sir Wisdom greeted them. "How went the battle?"

"The enemy attacked in force, my lord," Paul replied, "but they were routed completely by the men of Mitspah."

Abruptly, the men all began talking at once, each determined to tell some aspect of the battle that he had witnessed. Sir Wisdom laughed as he held up his hands to quiet them. "Gentlemen, gentlemen, please! I won't understand a word if you all speak at once. Save your tales to tell to your wives and children. They will be fascinated by your stories, I assure you."

His keen gray eyes scanned the group of men. "Gentlemen, you now see the importance of completing the Castle of Hope. The battle that you have just witnessed is still in the future, of course, but it will take place. Mitspah must be prepared. I hope that tonight after viewing the battle you now have a sense of urgency to finish the castle for the safety of your families and for the glory of Emmanuel."

The old nobleman paused and studied the faces of the men before him. "Men of Mitspah, are you ready to resume work on the Castle of Hope? Are you ready to see the castle project through to completion?"

Silence greeted him.

Sir Wisdom glanced at his sister and then turned his unwavering gaze back to the villagers. "Men of Mitspah, time is of the essence! The castle must be completed, and soon! The battle that you just witnessed is in the future, of course, but if it had taken place in your village this afternoon, the outcome would have been far different. May I remind you that your castle is not completed? The village walls are not even built. Surely you don't think that you and your families are ready to face an assault by Argamor's forces!"

The villagers stood silent, shifting restlessly, most of them looking at the ground as the old man spoke. Suddenly, Sir Wisdom was angry. "What keeps you from His Majesty's service?" he raged. "What could possibly be of greater importance to you than building the Castle of Hope to protect yourselves and your families against the attacks of your malevolent adversary, Argamor? Why do you not see that the castle must be built, and must be built now?"

Stony countenances greeted his words.

He stepped closer to the group of men, so angry that he was trembling. "Men of Mitspah, is it the golden lamps? Can it be possible that those worthless glittering lamps are so alluring that you will sacrifice your families and your futures in the hopes of obtaining one? Gentlemen, I remind you that any man who owns a golden lamp will forfeit it immediately when King Emmanuel calls you to the Golden City of the Redeemed."

Sir Wisdom stood quietly for several long moments gazing intently at the group of men before him. Tension filled the air.

At last, the old man stepped to the dying fire and began to add more wood. He watched for a moment as the flames leaped up hungrily. Turning himself about, he spoke. "Prince Josiah," he said quietly, "take these men back into the Lake of Destiny. There is yet another battle that they must witness."

Chapter Seventeen

The somber group of villagers followed the young prince back into the swirling waters of the Lake of Destiny. Without hesitation they waded out deeper and deeper until the waters closed over their heads. A moment later there was a sudden flash of light and the group found themselves back on the narrow trail in the forest. After a hike of several minutes they made their way out of the woods and paused once again on the mountainside above the village of Mitspah.

"Look," one villager blurted, "the castle is not finished."

"Aye," said another, "but the houses on top of the ridge are."

"We're about to witness another battle," Prince Josiah told the men, "and unless I miss my guess, we're about to see what will happen to the village if Argamor attacks before the Castle of Hope is completed."

As he spoke, a company of horsemen arrayed in dark armor galloped over the crest of the hill to the north and rode down upon the village. At the same moment a huge company of infantrymen approached from the south while pike men and archers attacked from the east. All wore dark armor that bore the red dragon of Argamor's coat of arms.

The gong in the village sounded the alarm, clanging again and again as it broadcast its desperate message. The villagers were in panic, knowing that they were not prepared for the attack and that there was no place to run. They had no place of refuge, no sanctuary. Men, women, and children scattered like helpless chicks fleeing from a hawk.

The horsemen reached the village before their counterparts. Cursing the name of Emmanuel as they rode, the dark knights raced through the narrow streets, using their swords and crossbows indiscriminately to slaughter any unfortunate who crossed their path. Others raced through the village with firebrands, laughing with ghoulish glee as they tossed burning torches onto thatched roofs in an attempt to destroy the village.

The men on the hillside were aghast as they watched the destruction of their homes.

Another group of dark riders rode furiously up the ridge toward the magnificent stone houses. Dismounting, they used their battle axes to demolish the doors of the houses and then entered to ransack the dwellings. Demas and the other lamp owners were beside themselves with rage.

"Wait! You can't take my son!" Barnabas screamed in fury as a handsome young lad was pulled screaming from his beautiful home on top of the ridge and thrown across the back of a horse. The dark knight leaped into the saddle and galloped from the ridge. Barnabas leaped to his feet, determined to make a desperate attempt to save his son.

Josiah seized him. "You can't stop him, Barnabas!" he cried, wrestling with the man to keep him from racing headlong down the mountainside. "You are in another dimension of time, and you cannot change the outcome of what is happening!"

"They can't take my son!" Barnabas screamed in fury.

Argamor's infantrymen had reached the village by this time. As the men on the hillside watched helplessly, the dark knights began to go from house to house, rounding up any children or youth that they could find and carrying them off as captives.

"No, no, no! Not Rachel! Not Jeremiah!" another father cried as his children were led from the village with their hands tightly bound. "You can't take my children!"

The men of the village watched in helpless fury as one by one their sons and daughters were led from the village as captives of the dark knights. It was a heart-rending scene. Weeping in fear as they were led away, the young captives begged for mercy, terrified at the thought of being separated from their families. But the dark knights were unrelenting.

The battle was over almost before it had started. The enemy forces vacated the valley as swiftly as they had come, leaving behind a burning village and a host of dead or wounded villagers. High atop the rocky promontory overlooking the village stood the unfinished Castle of Hope, empty and useless.

Prince Josiah turned to the men of the village. "Let's...let's go back, men," he said soberly, struggling with the words.

The moon was high in the heavens as the weary group emerged from the waters of the Lake of Destiny. The men trudged back to the bonfire and dropped to their knees in the grass, heads down, completely devastated by the horrors they had witnessed.

Sir Wisdom and Lady Prudence approached. "Men of Mitspah," Sir Wisdom greeted them. "How went the battle?"

Some of the men around the fire began to weep.

Sir Wisdom waited quietly.

"You know what happened, sire," one man shouted in fury. "We watched as our village was destroyed and our children were taken captives! You knew what was going to happen!" Sobbing, he sank to the ground and collapsed, overcome with emotion.

"It was as though our very lives were being torn apart right before our eyes," said another.

"Our children were taken by the enemy and we were helpless to stop it," a third man sobbed. "There was nothing we could do to change the outcome of the battle!"

"Would you have changed the outcome if you could?" the nobleman asked softly.

"Aye, sire, we would," a dozen voices chorused.

"If this battle takes place before the Castle of Hope is completed, the outcome will be just as you have witnessed, and it will be too late to change it," Sir Wisdom quietly told the men. "The time to change the outcome is now.

"Tonight you had the opportunity to find out for yourselves what Argamor really wants. Gentlemen, he wants your children, and he'll stop at nothing to get them. He plans to take your children captive that he might destroy their lives, their souls, their futures. The battle for Mitspah is a battle for the souls of your children."

He paused for several long moments to allow his words to take effect. The men before him sat or knelt around the fire, heads down, many sobbing or weeping openly, thoroughly spent emotionally by the massacre they had just witnessed.

Finally, Sir Wisdom spoke again. "Men of Mitspah, the outcome of the future battle is in your hands. Go back to your homes and families and build the Castle of Hope for the sake of your children. Set aside anything and everything that would hinder you from finishing the work to which His Majesty has commissioned you. The castle must be completed! You must be ready when Argamor attacks!"

"Sire, my golden lamp has kept me from working on Emmanuel's castle," Barnabas said, wiping his eyes. "What shall I do with it?"

"Cast it into the river, if that is what it takes," Sir Wisdom replied gently, "but do not allow it to draw you away from serving your King or protecting your family in the coming battle."

"The lamp shall be hurled into the river at first light tomorrow," Barnabas promised fervently. "I will do my part to change the outcome of the battle that we have just witnessed."

A chorus of voices gave assent to his decision.

"How many of you will be on the work crews tomorrow?" Sir Wisdom asked quietly.

Without exception, every man stood to his feet. Sir Wisdom beamed. Master James was overjoyed.

"Stand firm in your decision," Sir Wisdom told the men. "Tomorrow morning when the sun comes up you may be tempted to seek the golden lamps just one more time. Your wives and even your children may question your decision and seek to dissuade you from it, but stand firm. When the castle is finished and your families have a place of refuge from Argamor's next attack, you will not regret your decision."

A branch in the fire broke in half with a loud snap, sending thousands of tiny sparks skyward like brilliant fireflies. Sir Wisdom looked upward. "Men of Mitspah, it's time to call the lepidopteras."

Chapter Eighteen

Prince Josiah followed Phillip through a dense canebrake. Walking painstakingly across mossy ground that quivered with their every step, they carefully skirted a fetid swamp and then started up a gentle slope.

"The Castle of Hope was a beehive of activity today," the young prince told the young huntsman. "You should have seen it. The entire village worked on the castle until late afternoon. I left half an hour ago to join you on this hunt and there were more than a hundred villagers still working."

"Praise the name of Emmanuel," Phillip responded. "Last night changed Mitspah forever, I reckon."

"As far as I know, there was only one man in the entire village who was not there."

Phillip lowered his bow and turned to face Josiah. "Demas?"

Josiah nodded.

Phillip shook his head sadly.

The two young men continued up the slope, climbing over boulders and fighting their way through dense brambles. "There's one bit of disturbing news," Josiah went on. "The saboteur is still at work."

The young huntsman snorted in disgust. "Will we never be rid of him? What happened?"

"The carpenters had begun work on the front gates," Josiah replied, "and some time during the noon meal, someone set fire to the timbers. By the time we reached the castle site, most of the timbers were engulfed in flames."

"The saboteur is getting mighty bold."

Josiah nodded. "Perhaps he'll get too bold and we'll catch him in the act."

Phillip suddenly froze. "Look!" he whispered. "The golden hart!"

The magnificent deer stood in a small grove of beech trees less than two hundred paces away.

Phillip's eyes shone with excitement. "He's upwind from us," he whispered, fitting an arrow to his bowstring, "and he's facing the other way. Today is the day! The golden hart will be mine!"

Dropping to a crouching stance, he crept through the tall grasses as he made way carefully toward his elusive quarry. Josiah followed at a distance, moving as quietly as possible. The hart's tail went up and his ears perked up. The young hunter froze. Josiah held his breath.

After a moment or two, the golden hart dropped his head and began to graze. Phillip turned to Josiah and grinned.

Moving slowly and cautiously, the young hunter crept to within forty paces of the huge hart. Dropping to one knee, he slowly pulled the bowstring to full draw. Josiah held his breath and realized that his heart was pounding with the excitement of the hunt.

At that moment, an old man in nobleman's dress appeared directly in front of the golden hart, raising his hands as if to stop Phillip's arrow. The young hunter was shocked. "Sir Wisdom!"

"Why do you struggle so hard to obtain that which will never be yours?" Sir Wisdom asked sternly.

Phillip stared at him. "I—I do not understand," he faltered, lowering his bow.

"Why do you hunt the golden hart when His Majesty has commissioned you to provide food for the workers at the Castle of Hope?"

"The golden hart will be food for the workers once I take him," Phillip replied.

Amazed that the magnificent hart had not moved, Josiah slipped down the hillside and stood a few paces from Phillip.

"Be honest with yourself, Phillip," the old man chided gently. "You do not hunt the golden hart for food; you hunt him for status."

"Status, sire? I do not understand."

"As you know, most of the villagers abandoned their work assignments at the castle in order to seek the golden lamps at the quarry. Do you know why the lamps were so alluring? Do you know why Emmanuel's followers, good men and women almost without exception, would abandon a project commissioned by their loving King and designed for their own good, in order to seek something else?

"The lamps brought prosperity, lad. The 'fortunate' ones who found lamps obtained prosperity almost instantly. They could now buy houses and lands and horses and rich clothing. Why are those things so attractive? Prosperity brings status, Phillip, feelings of importance and significance. The real attraction of the golden lamps was that they brought status to those who found them."

Sir Wisdom paused and looked kindly at the young huntsman. "To your credit, my young friend, you resisted the allure of the golden lamps when nearly everyone else in the village was affected. You stayed faithful to your King in spite of the desire for wealth that lives within the breast of every one of Emmanuel's subjects."

He sighed. "So Argamor influenced you in another way."

Phillip frowned. "I don't understand, sire. I have stayed faithful. I have hunted nearly every single day since work started on the castle."

The old man nodded. "Indeed you have. But tell me—how many harts or pheasants or roebucks have you put on the village tables in the last three weeks?"

Phillip took a deep breath. "None, sir. But I have been hunting this magnificent hart. He's the biggest one I've ever seen, sire. Imagine how many meals he will provide when I take him!"

"You have been hunting every day, yet you have not provided a single meal for Master James' staff or the villagers in the past three weeks. Do you not see what has happened? Argamor has distracted you from service to your King."

To the amazement of the two young men, Sir Wisdom walked over and passed his hand through the body of the magnificent hart. The animal faded from view. "The golden hart is an illusion, Phillip. He represents excellence. Excellence beyond what King Emmanuel has planned for you."

A bewildered look appeared on the young huntsman's countenance.

"You strive for excellence in everything you do, and that's a commendable trait. When you learned archery, you became the finest archer in the region. When you learned to hunt, you became the most skilled huntsman on this side of Terrestria. Whatever you set your hand to, you determine to excel at it."

"Is it wrong to seek to be the best?"

"Why do you seek to be the best?" Sir Wisdom asked gently.

"Do you seek to be the best for the honor of Emmanuel? Or do you seek to be the best to glorify yourself? Excellence for the sake of excellence often becomes a matter of pride, my friend, and pride never glorifies the King."

He paused. "Let me see if I can explain this in a way that will make sense. When you first saw the golden hart, you determined that you would be the one to take him. Why? To provide food for the tables of Mitspah? Nay, for any two mature harts would provide more food than this one, yet you have spent more time seeking the golden hart than it would take to bring home forty harts.

"So why did you seek the golden hart? Simply for status, Phillip. No one else in the village has ever taken so magnificent an animal as this. What an impression it would make on the villagers, and on Rebecca, if one day you rode into the village with a hunting trophy almost too big for your horse to carry!"

The old man smiled in a benevolent way. "Have I told the truth, Phillip?"

The young huntsman hung his head. "Aye, my lord. I—I suppose I haven't seen it this way, but everything that you said makes sense, and I see it now."

"Forget about impressing the townspeople, Phillip. Forget about impressing that young lady by the name of Rebecca—though I must say that she is quite impressed with you already. Simply seek to be what His Majesty has planned for you; be the best huntsman that you can be, no more."

Phillip nodded. "Aye, sire. Thank you, sire."

In the next few months the work on the Castle of Hope progressed rapidly. The outer curtain was quickly finished and work resumed on the towers. The carpenter crew labored diligently to build the drawbridge, the main gates, and the gatehouse. A second crew of stone masons worked rapidly to complete the town wall while the carpenters constructed the gates. The people of Mitspah once again threw heart and soul into the castle project and the work went forward at a rapid pace. Many of the townspeople who had found golden lamps now used their wealth, or portions of it, to build the castle. Emmanuel's work had indeed become a priority.

One evening Prince Josiah stood on the sentry walk in the newly completed northwest tower of the Castle of Hope. The castle lay below him, glowing pink and amber in the rays from the setting sun. He turned and surveyed the village of Mitspah. He could see the flickering glow of cooking fires in the village below and knew that most of the villagers were preparing for the evening meal. Hearing the tread of footsteps on the spiral stairs below, he realized that someone was coming up into the tower with him. He waited.

Master James appeared and joined him on the sentry walk. "The castle looks magnificent at sunset, does it not?" the engineer commented. "This is my favorite time of day."

"It's mine, too," the young prince agreed.

Master James heaved a long, contented sigh. "It's good to see the castle nearing completion, isn't it? Prince Josiah, I am grateful that you were willing to come to our aid. But for you, perhaps the Castle of Hope would never be completed."

"I am grateful that I could serve Emmanuel in this way. I am grateful that His Majesty could use me."

"He has used you, my prince, and I am grateful." The master engineer paused. "Josiah, could I ask you to do the village of Mitspah a huge service?"

"Anything, sir."

"I know that you're a busy man, my lord, but I need your help."

"Name it, sir."

"As you know," Master James said, "His Majesty sent a shipment of swords and armor some time ago. They have been placed in the hands of the villagers, but the people still have not learned to use them. I know that they showed no interest when you first offered to teach them, but all that has changed now. Would you be willing to teach a class on swordsmanship, perhaps one evening a week? Phillip has agreed to teach a course in archery, and Paul is planning to teach on castle defenses and strategies of warfare. I am told that no one handles a sword as you do, and I thought that perhaps..."

"Let us plan on it," Josiah interrupted. "I'd be delighted to help the villagers prepare in this way, and I'm thankful that they're now ready to learn. Simply choose a time and a location, and I'll be there."

"I am grateful," Master James replied. "We will start classes next week. The villagers are determined to be ready to defend their homes and families in the event of an attack."

The two were silent for several moments as they enjoyed the sunset and the evening breezes. Josiah watched as a light appeared in the magnificent house on top of a distant ridge. "Demas is determined that he and his family will remain in their new home, isn't he?"

Master James nodded. "He worries me. All the others who were building on the ridge have realized the danger of building so far from the castle. They have dismantled their homes and are rebuilding within the safety of the town wall, but Demas still insists that he and his family will be safe on top of the ridge. I wish he would listen to reason."

He turned to go. "Prince Josiah, thank you again for coming

to the Castle of Hope. You have been a help to the people and a real encouragement to me."

Work started on the inner curtain wall the very next day. Master James' staff and the villagers worked so energetically that within a week the north wall had reached a height of fifteen feet. The carpenters completed the inner gates in just a few days and then started construction of the great hall and the other buildings within the inner bailey.

Early one morning, Josiah joined the crew of stone masons and worked atop the inner curtain wall. As the crew paused for a rest break, Master James came over to the young prince. "The saboteur is at work again," he quietly told Josiah. "What can we do to catch him?"

"What happened?" Josiah wanted to know.

"The chains that raise the drawbridge have been cut," the engineer responded with a sigh, "allowing the counterweights to drop down into the recesses. It will take a good day's work to raise the weights and reattach them."

"Leaving the castle vulnerable until the chains are repaired," Josiah commented. "Until the repairs are made, the drawbridge cannot be raised."

Master James nodded.

"Double the guard," the young prince suggested. "This may mean that we are about to be attacked."

"I thought of that and doubled the guard already," Master James replied. He sighed. "If only we could figure out who the saboteur is! He works right under our noses without leaving a clue. Do you have any idea how we can catch him?"

"The only thing I know is to send another petition to King Emmanuel," Josiah replied.

"Excuse me, my lords." A slender young man carrying stone mason's tools attempted to pass them on the wall. Master James and Josiah stepped to one side to allow the youth to pass. "Thank you, my lords."

Josiah glanced at the face of the youth and then felt his pulse quicken. Drawing his sword, he brought the blade to bear on the young man's chest. "Not another step or I'll run you through!"

The youth's eyes were wide with terror. "My lord!" The tools clattered at Josiah's feet.

Master James stared in astonishment. "Prince Josiah, what—"

"Sir, I give you the saboteur of the Castle of Hope. This is the man who has committed all the treachery against the castle."

A strange look appeared on the engineer's face. "Josiah, you must be mistaken! Jason has worked faithfully with us every day since the beginning of the castle project and often helps with guard duty. On two separate occasions in the last few weeks I have sent him on special trips all the way to Arwyn to obtain special items that I needed. He would never sabotage the Castle of Hope!"

"His name is not Jason," the young prince replied, continuing to hold the prisoner at bay with his sword, "and he is not one of the villagers as you suppose. I have had dealings with this blackguard before. His real name is Discouragement, and he serves as an agent of Argamor."

"But he is just a youth!"

"Take a closer look," Josiah advised. "Look into his eyes. Discouragement is older than you and me together, though he feigns himself as a younger man."

The engineer shook his head in disbelief. "What shall we do

with him? Do we kill him?"

"I wish that were possible, though I'm afraid it is not. Parade him before the villagers so that all will know who he is, and then lock him in the castle dungeon. I dare say he will escape before much time has passed."

Chapter Nineteen

"The house is beautiful, my love," Rebecca called up to Phillip, who sat astride the ridgepole of the little cottage. "It's just beautiful!"

Phillip laughed. "Well, it will be when it's finished, darling, but right now it doesn't even have a roof!" He swung down from the ridgepole, dropped lightly to the earth, and then came over to stand beside her. "Now that the Castle of Hope is finished, I've had more time to work on our place."

"It seems like a dream, doesn't it?" she said happily. "I still cannot believe that Father gave you permission to marry me. Just one month, and we'll be together in this beautiful house."

"Just one month and you'll belong to me," he replied joyfully, "and I'll belong to you."

"Oh, Phillip, I can hardly wait."

"The day will be here before we know it," he told her. "I still have a lot of work to do on the house."

At that moment, the village gong began to sound. Rebecca looked up with a puzzled expression. "Why is someone ringing..."

"An attack!" Phillip exclaimed. "Quickly—to the castle!"

Terror swept across her face. "We have to warn Mother and Father!"

"They'll hear the gong," he reassured her. "Our responsibility right now is to run to the castle."

As the gong continued to sound, an unusual peace reigned in the village of Mitspah. The villagers calmly gathered their families and made their way to the castle, hurriedly but without panic. Phillip escorted Rebecca safely to the castle and then gathered his company of archers and led them to positions atop the village wall.

A company of horsemen arrayed in dark armor galloped over the crest of the hill to the north and rode down upon the village. At the same moment a huge company of infantrymen approached from the south while pike men and archers advanced from the east. All wore dark armor that bore the red dragon of Argamor's coat of arms.

The vast army of Argamor's dark knights converged on the village of Mitspah. Phillip and his company of archers sent a barrage of arrows into the ranks of the enemy in an attempt to hold them at bay until the last of the villagers had reached the safety of the castle. A score of dark knights produced a battering ram and set to work on the town gates while a fusillade of arrows rained down upon them, killing some and wounding others. After losing a number of their comrades, the dark knights abandoned the battering ram and fell back.

Enemy troops with scaling ladders moved into position and placed their ladders against the village wall. Dark knights with swords drawn rushed up the ladders and gained access to the top of the wall. Phillip and his men drew swords and swiftly fought them back, completely clearing the walls.

Paul joined Prince Josiah on the battlements of the castle. "We haven't lost a single man," he commented, as he watched the battle for the village wall. "They've already lost scores of men."

"We fight with the weapons given to us by Emmanuel," Josiah replied. "Victory is assured when we battle in his might."

Atop the village wall, Phillip saw that the townspeople had all made it safely into the castle. "To the castle, men!" he shouted. "Hold the castle for the honor and glory of Emmanuel!"

The archers retreated to the safety of the castle. Mere seconds after the last of the archers crossed the drawbridge into the castle the constable closed and barred the massive main gates. The portcullis came slamming down and the draw-bridge was raised, sealing off the entrance to the castle.

Scores of dark knights screaming with rage suddenly rushed forward and swarmed up the scaling ladders, taking possession of the village walls. They unbarred the gates and opened them. The remaining companies of evil forces flooded into Mitspah and rushed toward the castle.

Time stood still. Prince Josiah, Master James and his staff and the men of Mitspah waged a spectacular battle for the Castle of Hope and the village of Mitspah. Wave after wave of dark knights assaulted the walls and gates of the castle time after time, only to be beaten back by the determined villagers bearing the weapons of King Emmanuel.

"Look!" an archer cried. "Demas and his family are outside the walls!"

All eyes darted to the ridge beyond the village. Three desperate figures could be seen running for the front gate of the village.

"They'll never make it!" Josiah lamented.

As the men of Mitspah watched in horrified silence, several dark knights bore down upon the wretched trio and ended the lives of the two adults. One of the dark knights seized the smallest figure and hoisted her over his head as if exhibiting a trophy.

"He has Mira!" Phillip screamed. "Josiah! We have to rescue her!"

"We'd need horses," the young prince replied miserably, knowing that the situation was hopeless. "How would we get horses across the moat? We dare not open the gates or lower the drawbridge."

"There are horses everywhere," Phillip replied. "I'll get us two!" Raising his bow, he shot an arrow over the castle wall, knocking an enemy knight out of the saddle. Seconds later, another dark knight tumbled from his saddle. "Two horses," Phillip said to Josiah. "Are you with me?"

Josiah nodded. "Let's go!"

Phillip and Josiah leaped over the castle wall to land in the moat, creating two tremendous splashes. They scrambled quickly to the side and dragged themselves out, drawing their swords as they did for they found themselves facing at least a score of dark knights.

"For the glory of King Emmanuel!" Josiah cried, rushing headlong into the throng of the enemy and swinging his sword furiously. Phillip was right beside him, fighting with equal ardor, and together they battled their way through the opposition to reach the two riderless horses. Mounting, they battled their way down the main street of the village until they reached the gate.

"Which way did they go with Mira?" Phillip cried, standing in his stirrups and looking about anxiously.

"There!" Josiah called, pointing. Mira's captor had thrown her across a horse and was attempting to mount. As he swung into the saddle she scrambled down, forcing him to dismount and start the process all over again. He threw her across the horse a second time, but again she slid to the ground as he mounted. Cursing, he drew back his fist to strike her.

Phillip's arrow caught the dark knight in the throat, striking him to the ground. Spurring his horse, Josiah rode forward, leaning down and calling, "Mira! Grab my arm!" She did as he rode past and in one fluid motion he jerked her up and across the saddle in front of him. Grabbing at his armor, Mira managed to sit up facing him.

"You'll be all right," Josiah assured the sobbing girl. She clung to him desperately.

Turning their horses, the two brave knights raced for the safety of the Castle of Hope. A number of dark knights saw them coming and rode into the street to cut them off. Wielding their invincible swords, Josiah and Phillip battled their way back toward the castle. "How will we get back inside?" Phillip called as they approached the moat. "They won't dare lower the drawbridge!"

At that moment, the drawbridge came crashing down. Fully two score of Emmanuel's knights came dashing out, battling furiously as they cleared the way for the culmination of the rescue. As the two horses dashed to safety, the knights fought their way back into the castle. With the crash of heavy chains and the whir of spinning pulleys, the drawbridge flew back up.

A resounding cheer filled the outer barbican of the castle as Josiah dismounted with his precious burden. Rebecca ran forward, seized the young girl, and hugged her tightly. "Oh, Mira, Mira!"

The battle for the Castle of Hope continued, but the villagers already knew what the outcome would be. Courageously they met and repulsed every assault of the enemy. At last, an enemy trumpet sounded the call to retreat and the dark knights ran for the hills, leaving more than half their number lying dead in the streets of Mitspah.

The men on the battlements raised a lively cheer. "All praise to His Majesty, King Emmanuel!" they exulted. "The village and the castle are safe! The victory is ours!"

Josiah felt a big hand on his shoulder and looked up into the face of Master James. "The outcome of this battle would have been far different," the big man said quietly, "had you not allowed His Majesty to use you here in Mitspah. Thank you for coming, and thank you for showing the townspeople the worthlessness of the golden lamps."

"I am thankful that His Majesty chose to use me," the young prince said quietly.

"Halloo the Castle of Hope," a voice called, and the two looked down to see a lone rider approaching the castle. The knight was arrayed in the armor of King Emmanuel. Chains rattled as the drawbridge was lowered to allow him access.

Moments later the strange knight made his way along the sentry walk. "I have a message for Prince Josiah of the Castle of Faith," he called.

Josiah stepped forward. "I am the one you seek."

The knight handed him a parchment. Josiah unrolled it and quickly read it.

"A message from His Majesty?" Master James asked.

Josiah nodded. "I am to return to the Castle of Faith," he replied. "Emmanuel has another mission for me." He turned to the messenger knight. "Thank you, sir."

The young prince made his way to the battlements above the main gate of the castle. "Good people of Mitspah," he called, "lend me your ear."

A hush fell across the castle. The townspeople moved close to the gate so that they could hear. All eyes were on Josiah.

"I must say farewell," Prince Josiah told them. "My father has called me away to the Castle of Faith in order that I may carry out another quest for his name. It has been my pleasure to get to know you and work with you. I implore you, stay close to the Castle of Hope and never forget its significance. Live your lives for His Majesty and seek to honor his great name in all that you do."

He paused and looked across the sea of faces in the barbican below him. "There is yet one thing that I must say before I take my leave. During my stay in the village of Mitspah I have heard constant use of the term 'peasant.' Most of you refer to yourselves in that way. Good people of Mitspah, you are not peasants, you are royalty!

"If you have put your trust in King Emmanuel and been set free from the chains of iniquity and the weight of guilt, as most of you have, you are children of the King! You are his sons and daughters!"

A murmur swept across the crowd of townspeople.

"My brothers and sisters, you are the children of the Lord of all Terrestria! I challenge you to live as royalty. Your father has promised to meet your every need; never return to groveling in the quarry, seeking the golden lamps of prosperity as the peasants of Terrestria would.

"One day very soon King Emmanuel will return and take us to live with him forever in the Golden City of the Redeemed. Good people of Mitspah, from this day forward, live as the children of the King!"

Glossary

Bailey: the courtyard in a castle.

Barbican: the space or courtyard between the inner and outer walls of a castle.

Battlement: on castle walls, a parapet with openings behind which archers would shelter when defending the castle.

Castle: a fortified building or complex of buildings, used both for defense and as the residence for the lord of the surrounding land.

Coat of arms: an arrangement of heraldic emblems, usually depicted on a shield or standard, indicating ancestry and position.

Curtain: the protective wall of a castle.

Doublet: a close-fitting garment worn by men.

Drawbridge: a heavy wooden bridge spanning the moat between the main gate and the surrounding land that could be raised to seal off the castle entrance.

Furlong: a measurement of distance equal to one-eighth of a mile.

Garrison: a group of soldiers stationed in a castle.

Gatehouse: a fortified structure built over the gateway to a castle.

Great hall: the room in a castle where the meals were served and the main events of the day occurred.

Inner curtain: the high castle wall surrounding the bailey or inner courtyard.

Jerkin: a close-fitting jacket or short coat.

Keep: the main tower or building of a castle.

Lance: a thrusting weapon with a long wooden shaft and a sharp metal point.

Longbow: a hand-drawn wooden bow $5^1/_2$ to 6 feet tall.

Lute: a stringed musical instrument having a long, fretted neck and a hollow, pear-shaped body.

Lyre: a musical instrument consisting of a sound box with two curving arms carrying a cross bar from which strings are stretched to the sound box.

Minstrel: a traveling entertainer who sang and recited poetry.

Moat: a deep, wide ditch surrounding a castle, often filled with water.

Mortar: a mixture of water, sand, and lime used to cement stones together.

Outer curtain: the outer castle wall surrounding the barbican.

Palisade: a sturdy wooden fence built for protection.

Portcullis: a heavy wooden grating covered with iron and suspended on chains above the gateway or any doorway of a castle. The portcullis could be lowered quickly to seal off an entrance if the castle was attacked.

Reeve: an appointed official responsible for the security and welfare of a town or region.

Saboton: pointed shoes made of steel to protect the feet of a knight in battle.

Salet: a protective helmet usually made of steel, worn by knights in combat.

Sentry walk: a platform or walkway around the inside top of a castle curtain used by guards, lookouts and archers defending a castle.

Solar: a private sitting room or bedroom designated for royalty or nobility.

Standard: a long, tapering flag or ensign, as of a king or a nation.

Tunic: a loose-fitting, long-sleeved garment.

Castle Facts

- The mortar used in castle walls was a mixture of water, sand, and lime.
- The inner and outer faces of each wall were constructed first.
- The spaces between the inner and outer faces were filled with rubble—a mixture of stones and mortar.
- In winter, construction on a castle was often halted because the cold temperatures tended to crack the wet mortar.
- The two most common openings in castle walls were windows and arrow loops.
- For security reasons the windows near the bottom of walls and towers were very narrow.
- Windows at the top could be quite wide.
- All windows were usually protected by an iron grille and could be closed with wooden shutters.
- The windows were the only source of natural light.
- In living quarters the windows were often fitted with glass.

The Priority of the King's Business

Just like the residents of the village of Mitspah, many times we fail to see the importance of the King's business, and we put other things first. As Josiah said, "Service to King Emmanuel brings rewards that will last forever, but anything else that we acquire will be taken from us the moment we leave for the City of the Redeemed." As children of the King, we must learn to put our priorities on the things that are eternal.

If you are not yet a child of the King, here's how to become one:

Admit that you are a sinner. The Bible tells us: "*For all have sinned, and come short of the glory of God.*" (Romans 3:23) Each of us has done wrong things and sinned against God. Our sin will keep us from heaven and condemn us to hell. We need to be forgiven.

Believe that Jesus died for you. The Bible says: "*But God commendeth his love toward us, in that, while we were yet sinners, Christ died for us.*" (Romans 5:8) The King of kings, the Lord Jesus Christ, became a man and died for our sins on the cross, giving his blood for us so that we can be forgiven. Three days later, he arose from the grave.

Call on Jesus to save you. The Bible says: "*For whosoever shall call upon the name of the Lord shall be saved.*" (Romans 10:13) Admit to God that you are a sinner. Believe that Jesus died for you on the cross and then rose again in three days. Call on Jesus in faith and ask him to save you. He will! And when he saves you from your sin, he adopts you into the royal family and you become his child—a prince or a princess!

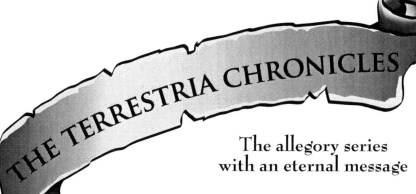